QUILTING WARRIORS:
Nedra & Lettie

Book 4 of The Bunco Club Series

ALSO BY KAREN DEWITT

The Bunco Club

Quilters of The Bunco Club: Phree & Rosa

Threads of Friendship: Marge & Beth

QUILTING WARRIORS:
Nedra & Lettie

Book 4 of The Bunco Club Series

Karen DeWitt

Karen DeWitt

Frame Masters, Ltd.
Matteson, Illinois 60443

Cover Photo by Robert M. DeWitt.

Published by Frame Masters, Ltd.
Matteson, Il 60443

ISBN-13: 978-0692675663 (Frame Masters, Ltd.)
ISBN-10: 0692675663

Printed in the United States of America.

To My Quilting Warrior Bunco Sisters
Thank you for over twenty-five years of friendship

Liz Collins, Sandy Concialdi, Bev Cooper,
Sandy Kowalski, Sharon Long,
Sandy Tedford, and Faye Van Drunen

List of Characters

Nedra Lange: Social Media Guru at the Mayflower Quilters Retreat, widow, mother of two college age daughters, Executive Assistant to Editor-in-Chief at *Excel Magazine*, African American, quilter, boyfriend (Nate)

Lettie Peabody: Fiber artist, single woman, quilter

Marge Russell: General Manager of the Mayflower Quilters Retreat, married (Bud), three children, control freak, quilter

Beth Stevenson: Salon owner/stylist, married (Tim), mother of three, hoarder, quilter

Phreedom (Phree) Clarke Eaton: Owner of the Mayflower Quilters Retreat, discovered valuable Mayflower documents, mother of Emily, divorced (Gary, aka The Bastard), quilter

Rosa Mitchell: Married (Terry), mother of Ricky and Alex, co-owner of The Pizza Depot with her husband, quilter

Helen Delaney: Married (Ben), mother of two, works at Quilter's Closet, quilter and long-arm quilter

Nancy Walsh: Single, boyfriend (Michael), learning disabilities tutor, quilter

Sunnie Eaton: Mother of Phree Clarke Eaton, Assistant General Manager of The Mayflower Quilters Retreat

Brian Barber: Brother of Nedra Lange, lawyer

Chapter 1
Lettie

Rosa hovered over the last pew in the chapel of the Mayflower Quilters Retreat, the MQR, as Marge rattled three dice in her cupped hands.

"Come on, Russell, you're killing me," Rosa said.

Marge rubbed the clattering cubes in her palms, brought her hands to her lips, and blew into a space between her thumbs. "Settle down, Miss Ants-in-your pants. You're the one who insisted on rolling first. I need to loosen up my wrists and get in touch with my lucky mojo if I'm going to stand a chance of beating you."

"You're having way too much fun torturing me. It's not fair." Rosa's bottom lip pushed out to resemble the pout of a stubborn three-year-old. "Besides, aren't you the one who's always reminding us to 'move along smartly'? I'm sure Nancy would love to find out who her maid of honor will be tomorrow."

Nancy tilted her head and shrugged. "No rush," she said. "I'm kind of enjoying this."

Rosa scowled. "Whose side are you on?"

Tomorrow afternoon Nancy Walsh, one of the Bunco Club women, would marry her long-lost love from twenty years ago. Of course she chose her closest friends, the other seven women from the Bunco Club, to be in her wedding. And of course she could not make the decision between who would be her bridesmaids and who would hold the top prize as maid or matron of honor. So of course it followed that there was only one way to solve the dilemma: Roll dice for the coveted position and also to determine the order of the bridal procession.

"I love you all equally," Nancy had told them. "There's no way I can choose one of you over the other."

And so it had been decided that on the night of the rehearsal dinner the seven women would roll three dice each. The highest tallied score would take the trophy as maid or matron of honor in Nancy and Michael's wedding ceremony the next day.

One unlucky roll of three snake eyes, and Lettie knew she didn't stand a chance to win the competition. "Three dice and I get a combined total of three. I guess we all know who will be first down the aisle," Lettie said. "Why can't I throw dice like this on Bunco night?"

When Rosa scored sixteen out of eighteen, and Marge and Helen were the only obstacles left to win the coveted positon, Lettie's dearest friend fist-bumped the bride-to-be.

"Way to go, Rosa," Nedra said. "Looks like you need to buy a lottery ticket tonight."

"Keep your sexy panties on, girls," Helen said. "I haven't had my turn yet."

The other women, some stifling giggles, looked toward the priest who stood off to the side with the other men observing this most unusual procedure.

Helen's face reddened. "Oh, God, sorry Father…oh no, I mean sorry twice…you know, one for the 'oh God' comment and one for the sexy panties thing. Oh, geez…"

Compressing his lips together to help maintain propriety, Father Murphy nodded, waved a hand, and said, "No worries, Helen. I've heard those words before. Continue."

Helen snapped her wrist and the dice bounced to a stop.

Rosa rocked on her heels and preened. "Looks like you're in the number two slot, right behind Lettie." Looking toward Marge, she said, "Now, for the final hurdle."

Marge lengthened the suspense by rubbing the dice between her palms.

"The quicker you ladies get this over with, the faster we can get on with rehearsal, and then head over to the retreat for dinner." Father Murphy patted his stomach saying, "I hear your head chef is planning something special and I, for one, am starving."

The onlookers agreed with smiles, head shakes, and an amen or two sprinkled in. Even though they would merely be walking across the MQR compound to the dining room, Helen jangled her key ring for effect.

"All of this dice throwing reminds me of the Bible story about gambling in the temple," the priest continued, "and if we don't get the show on the road, I might be tempted to share my views about Matthew 21:12-13 with everyone."

With that announcement, the dice shot from Marge's palm as though propelled by the wrath of God Himself. Clattering on the polished oak pew, one die teetered on the curved edge and stopped a smidgen before tumbling to the floor.

"The threat of a mini-sermon does it every time." Father Murphy chuckled under his breath.

Eight heads jockeyed to get a closer view of the three white cubes with black dots as the dice danced and bounced before slowing to a standstill on the wooden seat.

A split second of total silence broke when Rosa groaned and Marge threw her hands over her head shouting, "Woohoo! I won. I'm the matron of honor."

"I must say, that was a remarkable dinner," Tom Murphy said as he pushed the dining room chair away from the table. "And thank you for sharing such an amazing story about the beginning of your retreat, Phreedom. It's very inspirational and from the little I've seen, I'd say you've made a remarkable transformation." Smiling, he added, "If you'll forgive the intentional pun, you have resurrected this aging convent into a thriving and happy community."

"It was a vision that haunted me for many years," Phree said. "A dream which I thought could never possibly come true, nonetheless an obsessive idea that kept me sane through some rough times."

The priest tented his fingers, tapping the tips together. "I had no idea that this old complex was so large. No wonder it took such a long time to find just the right buyer."

"We're all fortunate to be part of this retreat," Lettie said, scraping the last of Chef Evelyn's homemade salted caramel ice cream from her bowl. "Phree is someone who would never 'toot her own horn' but she has been very generous to include her friends in all the fun and excitement this retreat has to offer."

Phree backhanded the air in front of her. "Pfshh," she said. "We're a team. Couldn't have done it without all of you."

Lettie knew that wasn't entirely true. Phree had recovered enough money from the sale of documents and items she found in an old family trunk to afford to do almost anything she wanted. She reminded her friends many times that the retreat didn't have to make money—that was what the interest on her investments was for. Rather the retreat simply had to break even every year. It was a means for Phree to live her dream and take her friends along for the ride of their life.

From the other end of the table Rosa craned her neck to see past the guests and called out, "Hey, Padre, wanna quick tour when we're finished eating?"

Lettie cringed. *Hey, Padre? Seriously Rosa, have some decorum.*

Father Murphy smiled. He meticulously folded his napkin, placed the linen square on top of the empty dessert plate in front of him, and said, "Sí, señora. But I must apologize, Rosa, that's about the extent of my Spanish."

"Then I'll be sure to keep my commentary in English."

Rosa tapped her napkin to her lips, wadded the cloth into a ball, plopped the crumpled bundle onto her plate, and stood. Motioning her hand toward the casually dressed priest with an 'after you' gesture and all the confidence of the Queen of the World, she said, "Shall we?" And then, switching back to her customary Rosa persona, she linked arms with the bride-to-be and called out over the casual chatter of rehearsal dinner guests, "Anyone wanna join us for a tour?"

"I'd love to join you," Sunnie said. "Phree, how about you?"

"I wish I could, but I'm going to help the other Bunco girls finish the decorating in the chapel," Phree said. "Since we've never transitioned from a quilting retreat to a wedding festivity before, I'm a little nervous about pulling this off. Even with all of our planning and Marge's meticulous organization, I want it to be perfect for Nancy."

"I'll try to get over there and help when the tour is finished." Patting her daughter on the back she told her, "Don't worry, hon. Knowing you girls and all the preparation we've done, it will be spectacular."

"Last call for the nickel tour," Rosa said. Several of the invited guests sidled over to the growing cluster of interested attendees.

A slim, white-haired woman adorned with contemporary jewelry tapped Nancy on the shoulder and said, "May I, dear?"

"Yes, of course, Gina." Nancy smiled at her future mother-in-law. "I was looking for you, but when I couldn't find you I thought you might have gone up to your room after dinner."

"I made a trip to the ladies' room...or should I say to the Poop Deck, where I ran into your mother. We had a nice chat."

Nancy's eyes went wide and her customary rash of heat rose from her neck and pooled in her cheeks. "Oh...oh, so you've met Adele? Was my sister with her?"

"I didn't see her," Gina answered. "It was just the two of us."

The bride to be sputtered, causing her cheeks to redden even deeper. "I hope my mom was...that is, did she say anything, um...that might have been, ah..."

Nancy had often described her mother as 'a piece of work.' Adele Walsh, who retired to the sunbaked state of Arizona, had a reputation of being a social-climbing friend-a-holic. The fact that her daughter was marrying a famous jeweler had sent Nancy's mother into a state of bragging ecstasy of epic proportions, which was 'unheard of in the whole wide world,' this according to Nancy. For several weeks the bride-to-be had been instructing, more like threatening, her mother through emails and over the phone to 'tone it down' at the wedding, especially around Michael's family.

"I'm not sure she can help herself. I truly think it's an addiction," Nancy said at Bunco one night. "If any of you are around when she starts being her annoying self, *please* step in and stop her. I'm begging you."

Lettie walked forward to rescue the awkward moment for her friend. At the same time she spotted Momzilla stepping out of the Poop Deck, head rotating like an owl, apparently looking for her new best friend, the mother of the groom. Interrupting Nancy's stuttering, Lettie said to Gina, "I couldn't help but overhear that you're Michael's mother. It's so nice to meet you. I'm Lettie Peabody, one of Nancy's Bunco and quilting friends."

"Both Michael and Nancy have talked a lot about her Bunco girls. It's a pleasure to meet you. Will you be joining the tour, too?"

"I'm afraid not. We've got some decorating to do in the chapel, but first I need to ask Sunnie a question." Lettie addressed the assembly of guests. "I don't want to appear rude, but this is a secret for you-know-who." She smiled and nodded toward Nancy. Taking hold of Sunnie's elbow, Lettie separated her from the group.

"What's up?" Sunnie asked.

"As you heard, Adele Walsh is about to join the tour. It appears as if she's attempting to get closer to Gina, as well as making Nancy even more stressed out than she already is. Stay with Mommy Dearest for the rest of the night and run interference for Nancy," Lettie said. "I'll tell the others you'll be at the chapel as soon as you can make it."

"Copy that," Sunnie said. "It looked as though Nancy was going to pass out after Gina said she had been chatting with her mother in the Poop Deck."

"If it wasn't so sad, it would be funny," Lettie said.

Walking backwards and employing her best Vanna White impression, Rosa steered the little group of attentive followers toward the Hannah Brewster Quilting Room. The last thing Lettie heard her friend saying was, "This is where all the quilty magic happens."

Chapter 2
Nedra

Over the past few weeks the bride's friends had gathered and assembled a collection of items they would use to decorate the chapel. Surreptitious meetings were held without Nancy's knowledge as plans were discussed, argued over, and finally decided upon. While attempting to honor Nancy's wish for a simple no-frills wedding, Nedra had to admit that preparations may have gotten a little out of hand — only by a smidgen though. As Rosa so succinctly put it, "Nancy's going to kill us when she sees what we've done."

The bounty of decorations was collected and stored at the MQR in one of the empty suites — a room where Nancy would have no business entering and therefore would remain clueless of their plans. Nedra, along with Helen, Marge, and Val (Marge's five-months-pregnant daughter) had spent a long afternoon organizing, sorting the items, and packing them in boxes, plastic bins, and bags for easy transport.

Parcels marked CHAPEL in red block letters sat on the wraparound porch near the entrance to the MQR, and were currently surrounded by the Bunco players who were *not* on Rosa's grand tour. The generous overhang of the porch roof protected packages and people from the falling snow.

"It looks like that storm they talked about is starting right on schedule," said Helen.

"And those are some honkin' huge flakes," said Lettie. "I heard the prediction is seven to ten inches depending if the lake-effect snow kicks in."

Several of the women let out groans. It had been a record-breaking December for snowfall and there were wagers and jokes that the mounds of plowed snow would still be melting by Memorial Day.

"Well, gals, Nancy's big moment has finally arrived," said Phree as she blew on her hands and then jammed them into the pockets of her coat. "I've never seen her glow like she did tonight."

"Where are your gloves, missy?" Nedra asked.

"I forgot them back home." Phree tilted her head toward the house across the compound where she lived.

Marge had apparently overheard the conversation and began to dig around in her purse. Moments later she thrust a pair of thin drugstore gloves at her friend. "Here ya go. I always carry a few extra pair with me in the winter for when I see a homeless person without gloves."

Phree reluctantly reached out and took them. "Thanks. I...I'll give them back so you can pass them along to someone."

"Good idea," said Marge.

Nedra had never met anyone quite like Marge Russell. Marge was an enigma—a dichotomy in constant motion. Nedra thought, not for the first time, that she might pattern a character after Marge for the novel she would soon be writing.

"I hear him coming." Excitement bubbled in Beth's voice with those four short words.

The head of maintenance, Steve Bonini, commandeered the John Deer Gator and its largest trailer up to the front door of the retreat. "Hey ladies, are we ready to rock and roll?"

"You bet," said Phree. "Let's do this thing."

"So many fun surprises," Beth said as she hefted a gray bin into the back of the trailer.

Warm breath puffed from the workers and formed short-lived clouds of steam that dissolved into the cold January night air.

Standing at the side of the green carrier, Steve said, "Hand those bundles to me, ladies. I'm used to packing this thing good and tight. Let's try to make one trip of it and get you out of this weather as quick as we can."

"You got it," Nedra said, as she passed him an oversized cardboard box. "Be careful with this one. It's the show stopper."

"What's in it?" Steve asked. "A hundred pounds of chocolate?"

"Smarty-pants," Phree said as she gave his shoulder a playful smack.

"We all need to make sure Nancy doesn't go anywhere near the chapel until the wedding tomorrow," Helen said. "You know how sneaky each of us can be when we think there's a secret that we've been left out of."

"All I can say is Nancy's going to be blown away when she walks down that aisle. I can't wait to see her face." Marge handed Steve the last package.

The Gator and its trailer were filled to the brim with miscellaneous-sized nondescript bundles. Steve crisscrossed and then buckled two black packing straps to secure the load in the trailer. "I've got room for two passengers," he said. "Any takers?"

Working her way to the backseat where there was just enough room to squeeze in between parcels, Helen said, "I'll hop on and we can get started unloading while the others walk over."

"Good idea. I'll come along and help unload, too," Lettie said.

Steve coaxed the Gator into a U-turn on the wide driveway and headed the precious cargo toward the chapel.

As the women trekked along the sidewalk across the compound to the chapel, Phree said, "It's a good thing most of the out-of-town people are staying right here at the retreat. A lot of them don't know how to drive in snow."

"Luckily, we're a full-service retreat with a shuttle that can get everyone to the airport on Sunday." Marge laughed. "Too bad we aren't shut down for all of January. We could sure use the time to recuperate and switch gears back to our beloved MQR."

The Gator crew had arrived at the chapel and turned on the indoor lighting. Nedra watched as a prism of diffused colors tumbled from the stained glass windows onto the fresh sparkling snow.

"You can't beat those fabulous windows," said Helen. "I'll bet you almost pooped when Lettie told you she suspected they were Tiffany."

Phree snorted. "That's an understatement. What are the odds? The appraiser will be here to check them out in February. I've got my fingers crossed."

Shaking her head Nedra said, "Girl, how lucky can one person be?"

"I'm glad we already got the Brewster Room and the rest of the main building ready for the reception and the guests," Phree said.

"Me too," Marge said. "Thank God this is the last decorating that needs to be done. I know I must have said this a million times, but I can't wait to see the look on Nancy's face tomorrow when she sees what we've done."

"It's going to be epic," Nedra said.

In the short time it took to walk across the MQR compound, the snow had increased in volume and the wind had picked up. Nedra drew her handmade scarf close around her collar in an attempt to keep the wet and cold from rushing down her neck. "Looks like they've almost got everything inside," she said. "I hope the furnace was left on after the rehearsal."

"We usually keep it just warm enough in the winter so the pipes in the washrooms don't freeze," Marge said. "It shouldn't take long to warm up."

"Come on, you slackers," Helen called. "We've almost got everything inside already."

"You mean you haven't finished decorating yet?" Marge joked, as the four walkers stomped snow off their feet under the protective canopy of the entrance to the chapel.

Nedra met up with Marge and shared a whispered comment behind their hands.

"That does it," Lettie said. "What's going on between you two? You two have been sharing too many private chitchats for my liking."

"Nothing," Marge said. "Really. We're just excited, that's all."

Steve broke into the conversation. "You ladies call me on the talkie if you need anything. I'm going to start maintenance on the sidewalks and driveways. We could get hit big by this storm and I don't want any casualties tomorrow when people are walking between here and the retreat."

"Will do," Marge, the General Manager of the Mayflower Quilters Retreat, said. "And good idea on the sidewalks. There'll probably be a lot of women in high heels making the hike."

Marge covertly discussed something with Steve, and Lettie sighed theatrically while throwing her hands in the air. "What the heck? Am I the only one seeing this obvious secrecy going on between Marge and other people?"

Marge shooed Lettie with her suspicions into the chapel, and Steve put the empty Gator into gear.

"When you're ready to go back to the main building let me know. I'll come and shuttle you back in two trips."

"Thanks," Phree said. "You're the best, Steve."

Cardboard boxes, plastic bags, and bins were scattered haphazardly in the entryway.

"It's an unorganized mess, but at least we got everything inside as fast as we could before it started coming down too hard," Nedra said. "We don't want to have to deal with soggy decorations."

Helen asked, "Where should we start?" And everyone

looked to Captain Marge.

"I think we should unpack all the quilts and walk them to the appropriate pews." Marge retrieved a sheet of paper from one of several file folders that she had hugged protectively to her chest while walking through the snow. "I've got the master drawing of where we thought they would best complement each other. Let's start by simply placing the folded quilts atop the armrests on the center aisle. That way it will be easier to switch them if we feel it's necessary to maintain visual perfection."

"By all means," Lettie said to tease their leader. "We must maintain visual perfection."

Pointing an index finger at her friend, Marge said, "Do you want to do this job, Ms. Peabody? Because if you want to spearhead this project, then it's all yours."

Lettie held up both hands shoulder high and palms out. "No, ma'am. I do not. I'm simply your smart-mouthed servant, here to do your bidding."

"That's better," Marge said. "But we can do without the smart mouth part."

Helen rose from bending over a tub. "If the two of you don't mind cutting the crap," she said, "the rest of us could use some help here." Two quilts were draped over one of her arms: one of Rosa's signature 1930s reproduction quilts and a wool appliqued beauty filled with summery images. "Let me see that chart."

Marge stood up from bending over a white plastic garbage bag with red ties. "Everybody stop what you're doing. We need to organize this process or we'll be here all night getting in each other's way." Marge walked toward a long table that was sitting empty in a corner. "Phree, help me with this." Marge pointed to where she wanted the table placed and continued talking as Lettie and Nedra grabbed the middle of each side. "Beth, Lettie, and Helen…you guys unpack the quilts and set them on this table. Using the chart,

I'll direct Phree and Nedra to the pew they belong on." Marge stood and brushed at loose hairs on her face. "Let's get going."

Nedra was pleased that Marge gave her the job to place the quilts on the pews. It was going to be fun watching the chapel warm up and come to life with their beautiful quilts as decorations.

The planning committee for the wedding, which was the whole Bunco Club except for Nancy, had spent the past several months bouncing ideas off each other. They whispered like spies with hands covering mouths as eyes darted around the room making sure Nancy was not within earshot. It was unanimously decided right away that quilts were to be the heartbeat of their design schemes; ideas ran rampant. At one point Rosa even joked that they should make their friend a quilted wedding dress.

The women narrowed down all of the ideas to the two best possibilities: Place quilts on the backs of the pews, or use quilts as a flourish on the ends of the pews. A compromise was struck when they concluded that with all of the quilters involved, there would surely be enough quilts to do both. Everyone walking into the church and down the aisle could admire the colorful quilts as they passed, and then be able to lean back on a soft folded quilt during the ceremony.

There were no armrests per se at the end of the pews. The ends were as tall as the backrest with large slabs of beautiful oak sporting an intricate peek-a-boo cutout design near the tops. The cutouts made the perfect way to pleat the quilts to prevent them from slipping off as guests entered and exited their seats. Sturdy strips of fabric had been artfully sewn by the group and would be guided through the cutouts and then tied in bows to steady the quilts in place. When all the work was done, the women were convinced it was going to look stupendous.

Pointing to a large quilt which was folded backing side out, Marge said, "Nedra and Phree, both of you carry this one next. Put it up by the altar."

"Ooooo, is this what I think it is?" Phree said.

Both women did as told and took hold of the massively large quilt, one person on either side. "Nancy's going to freak out when she sees this, and knowing Nancy like we do, she's not going to want to stand on it."

"Well, she's going to have to if she wants to get married," Nedra said. "That's what we made it for."

"Also for their bed," said Phree. "Don't forget that little detail."

When the convent was sold, all holy objects such as the altar and tabernacle, statues, communion cups, altar linens and the like were removed from the property. Nancy and Michael decided there was no need for an altar since they would not be having a Mass. "The priest will marry us, say a short preachy-type thing, and then off we go," said Nancy.

Over the top of the bundle they carried, Nedra said to Phree, "I really want to look at this quilt...and I mean *now*."

"Me too," said Phree. "Do you think we could get it unwrapped before Marge ran up here and killed us?"

"You know she would," Nedra said. "I suppose it's only fair that we wait for Rosa to get here."

"Yeah, knowing her she's probably schmoozing it up with the guests and eating more dessert while we do all the work," Phree said.

They were about four feet from the steps that would have led up to the altar if there was one, when Marge's voice boomed from the back of the chapel like an on-high command—her first few words punctuated for effect: "DON'T YOU DARE unwrap that quilt, ladies. We'll do that last and when we're all together."

Phree pressed her lips and lowered her head to hold in a laugh, but when Nedra yelled back, "Aye, aye, Captain," Phree let go with the biggest raspberry motorboat laugh Nedra had ever heard and then started laughing herself.

"Oh no," Nedra said. "I've gotta pee."

Phree crossed her legs and tried to walk. "I think I just did."

"Well, I must say this is beautiful," Marge said hours later. She clapped her hands together entering the oversized service closet near the entrance of the chapel. The room had once been used as a cloakroom for visitors and a convenient place to store folding chairs. "Nancy's going to be so flabbergasted and downright happy tomorrow."

Nedra wondered how Marge could still have an excited gleam in her eyes at the ungodly hour of 1:15 a.m.

The utility closet had been transformed, as if by miracle, into a plush waiting area for the bride and her attendants. Earlier in the week Marge had handpicked some comfy chairs throughout the retreat and earmarked them to be moved to the chapel along with a coffee table and a few end tables. A lush area rug was measured, rolled up, and sent over as well.

The women had emailed pictures of Nancy and Michael which they had on their computers to Nedra. She did her artistic best to manipulate the mementos into black and white images and then she inserted them into easel-backed frames. Several framed photos of the future bride and groom rested on quilted table toppers. Boxes of tissue were sprinkled around the room in strategic places. Awaiting the women when they arrived at the chapel tomorrow would be a few simple treats, compliments of Chef Evelyn, and a cart with wine.

It was nearing two a.m. and they were finally finished.

The friends clustered together in the silent vestibule of the long unused chapel that resided at the center point of the Mayflower Quilters Retreat compound. Lettie and Helen each placed an arm behind the other's back as Nedra rested her tired head on Marge's shoulder. The other women followed suit by linking arms or holding hands.

"Well done, ladies," Captain Marge said. "Let's get that Gator over here so we can head back to the retreat and get some much needed sleep."

Chapter 3
Lettie

Lettie woke to the sound of whirring snowblowers, shovels scraping the hard-to-reach parts of the sidewalks, and clanking snowplows clearing driveways and parking areas. The large wet snowflakes that had fallen relentlessly throughout the night began to lessen in size and intensity, and as if on cue, stopped altogether just after ten the next morning. The MQR maintenance crew had approximately three hours to clear, salt, and declare the walkways safe for the guests and bridal party.

Lettie was in on a secret and the snowfall had played right into the plans.

About a month ago she had been working silently beside Marge and Sunnie in the Bridge when Steve Bonini rapped on the doorframe and asked, "Hey Cap, got a minute?" Steve had dubbed Marge Cap...short for Captain.

"You bet," Marge said. "Come on in. Take a seat. What's up?"

With curiosity piqued, the three women stopped what they were working on and stared at the young man as though he was about to announce the secret to eternal youth.

"You know the large shed that I've had the crew cleaning out so we could use it for overflow storage?"

Marge nodded.

"We finally got to the back of it. It was mostly full of random stuff that someone probably didn't have the authority to throw away so they just kept shoving it in there. Anyway, look what we uncovered." Steve tapped his phone and the three women's heads hovered close together above the image on the screen.

Marge gasped and splayed her hand at her throat. "Oh my God."

"Wowzer," said Sunnie. "I wasn't expecting that."

"You've got to be kidding," Lettie said. "Why in the world would a convent ever need one of those?"

Steve shrugged and said, "I don't know. I guess sometimes nuns just like to have fun like everyone else."

"What kind of shape is it in?" Marge asked as she sat back down on her chair.

"Not bad," Steve answered. "It was covered in several tarps, so I guess that helped keep it clean at least. We haven't taken it out of the shed and inspected it, but my guess is it would probably be usable."

"Yeah, if we only had a few horses," Sunnie said.

"That gives me an idea." Marge tapped a finger to her lips. "Close the door, Steve, and let's discuss this further."

In the end it was Marge's idea that if there happened to be snow on the ground for Nancy and Michael's wedding day, the guests and bridal party would be shuttled to and from the chapel in a horse-drawn sleigh.

"It seats six people. I have no idea whether it would take one or two horses to pull a carriage that size. But Rob should know." Steve explained that his car mechanic owned some workhorses and that he could contact Rob if Marge wanted him to do so.

"Let me know when you get to a point where I can take a look at the sleigh. If it's in good enough shape, we'll move forward with our little surprise."

Later, Steve reported that one big draft horse would be all that was needed for the job. After discussing the cost, Rob agreed to hold the date open for his largest horse, Dakota. Lettie, Sunnie, and Marge were tasked with decorating the sleigh and horse.

"We could make some quick Christmassy lap blankets for the guests," Sunnie said. "I'll get some flannel fabric. We'll keep it simple...make a bunch of four-patches and join them together. It'll be pretty and festive."

"I love it," Lettie said. "Maybe a feathery plume for the horse's head would be cool, and wedding bells around its neck instead of sleigh bells."

Practical Marge said, "Now all we need is some snow."

And snow it had—seven and a half inches of the heavy packing variety, perfect for a wintry sleigh ride.

It was time for Nancy and her attendants to head to the chapel.

The women had done a tactful job keeping visits from Momzilla and Sisterzilla to a few short interruptions with comments like, "Nancy is so excited for both of you to be amazed by all of her planning. I'm sure you don't want to spoil her special surprises, so we've promised her that we won't let you see anything yet."

Beth had been kept busy fussing over everyone's hair. When the bride's updo was at last flawless, the tired stylist collapsed into the nearest chair. Nancy had held firm to her decision not to involve a makeup person for the big day and all of her friends were inclined to agree. They had relented, however, to allow Beth to 'work a little of her magic' here and there.

Lettie took pictures while Marge bothered over all manner of details, barking orders to anyone in her path. Rosa, Lettie, Helen, and Phree intermittently took turns pacing around the suite.

Sunnie tapped on the door and walked in the room. "Okay, ladies, it's time to do this."

"Oh, God," Nancy said.

Rosa petted her friend's arm. "You'll be fine, sweetie. Everyone gets a little nervous on their wedding day."

"Listen up, ladies." When no one stopped talking, Sunnie clapped her hands to get their attention. "Even with the snow shoveled, blown, and plowed to death by Steve and his crew, it's still pretty sloppy out there. So rather than walk and get those beautiful dresses and shoes wet, we've arranged for you to be transported in a vehicle to the chapel."

The women bobbed their heads and agreed that this was a good plan.

"The vehicle holds six people so we'll start with the bride, her matron of honor, and four volunteers," Sunnie said. "The rest of us can go in the second trip. All the guests have been driven over as have the groom and his party."

Lettie thought Sunnie was doing a remarkable job of remaining calm while at the same time pulling off their big secret.

"Let's all head downstairs," Sunnie said. "It's time."

Nancy whimpered.

Greg, the wedding photographer, clicked photo after photo of the women as they descended the staircase which was adorned with a garland of silk flowers. Sunnie had headed down in the elevator to further orchestrate the special departure, while Lettie and Marge nudged and elbowed each other behind the bride as they stifled giggles.

With authority, Greg called out, "One group picture in front of the stairway, please."

After the camera click echoed in the tall space, the group relaxed shoulders and started toward the door.

"Hold on," Sunnie called and held up her arms. Continuing to speak in her loudest voice she said, "Nancy, we know that you didn't want anything to do with a chauffeur today, but considering the weather and your beautiful dresses we had to come up with something. We hope you find our solution acceptable."

Lettie watched as heads turned with bewildered looks to see if anyone knew what in the world was happening.

"Follow me, ladies." Sunnie linked arms with Nancy, and the rest of the wedding party fell in line behind them—

buddy style—with Lettie and Marge bringing up the rear.

Marge squeezed Lettie's hand when the first shrieks of disbelief reached their ears. Within a moment they stood among the shocked group of friends. Nancy was frozen in place, both hands pressed firmly over her gaping mouth. Lettie saw the look of sheer wonder and happiness on her friend's face. She felt her eyes start to water but willed them not to leak—it wouldn't do to ruin her makeup.

Embellished with brass fixtures and bright-red trim, the deep mahogany body of the sleigh displayed a highly polished mirror finish. Three rows of soft leather seats were adorned with dime-sized brass tacks. Six folded lap quilts, assembly lined yet lovingly made by Sunnie, Marge, and Lettie, rested on the benches for each of the passengers.

The scene was like a modernized version of a Currier and Ives lithograph.

At the head of the sleigh was a magnificent and huge American Shire horse, pawing the ground with a feathered foot and snorting steam from his nostrils. Excited to be working and eager to proudly pull another full sleigh of people through the gleaming snow, Dakota tossed his head, and wedding bells around his neck tinkled while a flowing white plume bobbed on his head.

A blonde woman, short and a little bit stocky, her back to the jovial passengers, held tight to the reins of the horse's bridle. The huge horse lowered his head to hers while she cooed and patted his neck.

But what caught Lettie's eye was not the sleigh or the horse. It was the driver...*or was he called a coachman?* Lettie had no idea but as she pondered the question, the man who was standing posed and smiling by the driver's seat nearly made her gasp. *Who was he?* She stopped staring long enough to realize her mouth was gaping and she slammed it closed. Thank God it had not been a full blown gape... she hoped that maybe it was only half of a gape.

Her friends were talking around her, but it came across like white noise as Lettie tried to remember the coachman's name. *What had Steve called him?* She easily remembered the horse's name was Dakota...*Ha, figures I'd zero in on the animal and not the human. Tall. About my age. Nice eyes – no, make that great eyes. I love that he's dressed in character, like a footman from Downton Abbey. Nice smile – no, make that great smile. Is that a tattoo peeking out from his collar? Great hands with fingerless leather gloves and a leather braided black bracelet on his wrist. What did Steve say he did...I can't remember. Nice – no, make that great body, with just the right amount of stubble on his face...*

Someone called her name and Lettie spun her head around to see Nedra smiling at her. "Huh?"

Her friend approached and whispered in her ear, "Looks like someone is a little infatuated with the driver."

Lettie came down to earth and turned away from the mesmerizing man. "With my luck he's married with three kids...or else he's gay. The blonde hanging with the monster-sized horse is probably wifey-poo."

Placing a hand on either side of her mouth to aid in creating maximum volume, Marge shouted, "Let's all scoot together so we can make it in one trip." She looked to the driver asking, "Is that okay or will it be too much weight for Dakota?"

"Dakota is a workhorse, ma'am. He could probably haul three full sleighs connected to each other and still be having fun."

Marge nodded and called out, "All in, ladies. We've got to get this bride to church on time."

It was going to be a tight squeeze to get all nine women, one wearing a wedding dress, into a six-person sleigh. Giggles and laughter were prominent as the friends wiggled themselves into the carriage. Lap quilts were shared or tossed over bare shoulders. When only Nedra and Lettie were left to squeeze into the sleigh, Nedra suggested, "Lettie, why don't you ride up front with Rob?"

Feeling as though she had time traveled back to fourteen years old, Lettie wanted to die on the spot. But before she could look at Nedra and shoot daggers from her eyes, she felt a hand grip her elbow and a deep male voice say, "It'll be my pleasure. Come with me, miss, your chariot awaits."

Speechless, Lettie allowed herself to be led by Rob to the front of the sleigh.

"Let me help you up," Rob said. "This seat is quite a bit higher than the sleigh itself."

"I'm fine," independent Lettie said. "I'll just use these steps and..." The first step had to be three feet off the ground and Lettie was wearing a pencil skirt with almost-stiletto heels.

"Hang on. Here we go," he said.

Lettie found herself hovering horizontal to the ground. Rob had picked her up in his arms, the way you hold a baby, and in one fluid motion stood her on the bottom step leading to the driver's seat.

"There we are," Rob said, then whispered, "and not a pretty hair out of place."

The women in the sleigh hooted at the scene they had just witnessed.

"I'm next," called Rosa.

Rob left Lettie for a moment as he went around to the back of the sleigh, checking that the passengers were secure and ready to depart. He reached in and straightened a quilt or two on various laps. The women laughed when he held one up, inspected it, and pretended to steal it by stuffing it under his coat before returning it to Sunnie.

He's a charmer. Definitely married. Why won't that woman turn around so I can get a look at her? Lettie knew she wasn't feeling jealous of the blonde, but simply curious.

Rob walked past the driver's bench and with a gentle hand, touched the blonde's shoulder. The woman turned and smiled up into Rob's perfect face.

Yep, just as I thought married.... Lettie stopped her train of thought when she got a good view of the mystery woman's face. She had almond-shaped eyes that were spaced far apart from each other. The tip of her tongue rested on the lower lip of her slightly open mouth, but she radiated a loving smile to Rob when he quietly spoke to her. Lettie could not hear what he had said, but the woman answered with a loud voice...forcing words around a thick tongue.

"It's easy cuz 'Kota loves me. He's a good boy and he's my friend."

Rob said something low that was whisked away on the breeze before Lettie could catch even one word. Behind her in the sleigh the bridal party was chatting and laughing, completely unaware of the intimate scene she was witnessing. Rob pointed to the stairs on the porch.

"Okay, Robbie, okay. Just like before. I'll sit and be good till you come back with 'Kota. Just like before." A final kiss to the horse's neck and the mystery woman walked clumsily through the snow toward the porch steps.

With three long steps and a graceful leap, Rob was in the driver's seat next to Lettie. He turned to the adoring masses behind him and with a questioning look on his face motioned to his coat.

"Take it off," Rosa shouted.

He stood and bending at the waist in a deep bow, he did just that. Before Lettie knew what happened, the top coat was spinning through the air over her head and came to rest on her shoulders.

Cheers broke out behind her and Lettie wondered when this humiliation would ever end.

As Rob sat down he quietly said to his passenger, "Don't mind me, I'm a bit of a ham."

"I hadn't noticed," said Lettie.

"Shall we, mademoiselle? Better hang on to the rail." He made that familiar clicking sound with his tongue that you associate with getting a horse to move, and with a small jolt they were off.

There was no other word to use than *exhilarating*. In no time Dakota was sprinting—or whatever the right word was— and Lettie was clutching Rob's warm coat to her throat. There was no way she could not smile.

"So you're Lettie. I'm Rob. Nice to meet you." He held out his hand and Lettie shook it. She appreciated that he gave her a firm handshake and not a fishy you're-a-woman-so-I-don't -dare-squeeze-too-hard shake.

She smiled. "Nice to meet you, too, Rob."

"Wanna have some fun?"

She wasn't sure what he meant and when she didn't answer he continued.

"Let's take the bridal party on a grand tour of the grounds. It's a beautiful day for a sleigh ride before a wedding."

She had to agree, but what Lettie really wanted to know was: *Who is the woman with Down syndrome?*

With cheeks and faces rosy and stinging from the cold, the friends chattered excitedly as Rob helped them out of the sleigh. They reassembled in the bride's chambers at the back of the chapel.

"How in the world did this sleigh thing come about?" Nancy asked. "And this room..." she held out an arm. "You guys thought of everything. It's perfect!"

"I think a lot of us would like to know the answer to how in the world a horse-drawn sleigh came into the plans...and particularly why *I* wasn't told about it," Rosa said.

Marge, Lettie, and Phree took turns recalling the big secret of 'sleigh gate' while everyone wrangled into a seat. Toward the end of the story, Sunnie opened the wine and started pouring it into tall wineglasses. She picked up the tray of glittering stemware and went around the room offering a glass to each woman.

"Hold off sipping or guzzling for another minute, gals," Sunnie said. "We need to toast our favorite bride before she walks down the aisle."

Marge, of course, led the toast. Glasses clinked, eyes became damp, and the wine was downed quickly.

"That sure warmed me up," Nedra said.

"Same here," said Phree, and others smiled in agreement.

"Can we have one more round?" Nancy asked. "I'd like to make a toast, too."

Sunnie walked the room, topping off the tall stemmed orbs. When she was finished, Nancy stood.

"I'll keep this short as I have two things I want to say. First and foremost, thank you all. From the bottom of my heart I thank you. I love you all so much. I don't know what..." She stopped to steady her voice. "I can't imagine my life without all of you. When I try it's lonely and sad...uneventful...but mostly unmemorable. So, short of carrying on until our mascara starts to run and we all look like raccoons, I thank you for your friendship and I look forward to making memories with you and loving each of you for the rest of my life." Nancy paused, raised her glass and said, "To friendship."

"Hear, hear!" Marge and Nedra said.

"To friendship," said the group.

"Amen," said Helen.

Glasses clinked again as some of the group swiped at damp eyes until Marge took charge.

"Well, I think it's time, ladies," said Marge. "We all need to..." and every single person mimicked Marge by calling out, "Move along smartly!"

"Smart-alecks," Marge answered.

"One more minute, everyone," Nancy said. "I have an announcement."

Lettie, along with everyone else, had no idea where this was going. Those who had already risen to leave returned to their seats as Nancy stayed standing in front of her friends.

She stared into the empty wineglass in her hand. After a long deep breath she looked up at her friends. "I can't think of a better time or place to share this," Nancy said. Smiling and resting a hand on her abdomen, she said, "I'm pregnant."

Chapter 4
Nedra

Nancy's announcement caused a ruckus that was heard all the way to the front of the church.

A few minutes later, Father Murphy burst through the door and asked, "What is going on back here? Is everyone okay?"

"We're fine, Father," a beaming Nancy answered. "I just told them about..." Nancy patted her tummy. "You know."

His arms fluttered in front of him, and Nedra could tell he was embarrassed. "Well, keep it down and let's get this show on the road. People are waiting and beginning to wonder if you've changed your mind."

"Not a chance," Nancy said.

"Then line up *now*, ladies," the priest said as he spun to leave, vestments flying behind him. "The organist is on her third round of hymns."

"I think he means business," Beth said to Nedra.

The seven friends walked down the aisle according to their roll of the dice. As matron of honor, Marge walked just before the bride. Nancy had insisted she walk down the aisle by herself, but both of her parents were to exit the pew and join her for the last few steps. "I know it's weird, but it's just what I want to do. I've been independent way too long to suddenly need my father to get me to the altar."

Nedra had thought it was more than weird, but she also knew that Nancy and her parents had some bad history. It was probably a miracle that she even invited them to the wedding at all.

Once the bridal party was finally assembled at the front

of the church, the organist hit the low notes that signaled the entrance of the bride: *dum da da dum, dum dum da dum.* The crowd stood, and Nancy walked around the corner and into sight with the first sound of *Here Comes the Bride.* It took her about three steps to notice the quilts and she stopped in her tracks. She put her non-bouquet-holding hand to her chest and her eyes went to the group of smiling friends gathered on the bride's side of the church.

Nedra caught Fr. Murphy's eye roll at yet another stop in the already late ceremony. *This is going to be one wedding he remembers for a while.*

Independent, Nancy was…or maybe she was just old enough to do whatever the heck she wanted as she made her way down the aisle. Not only did she stop to pet and admire several quilts along the way, but she even reached into pews for hugs and well wishes.

Standing fourth in line of the bridesmaids, Nedra knew how difficult Nancy and Michael's journey had been to get to this point. Her heart swelled with pride that Nancy had the courage to make her own rules…even for walking down the bridal aisle.

The meetup with Mom and Dad at the end of the pew was chilly. It appeared that Nancy had been correct not to involve her family any more than she had to.

As they stood side by side, the priest asked, "Who gives this woman in marriage?"

Nancy answered. "I give myself to this man."

Nedra watched as a deep sigh emanated from Adele Walsh and was accompanied by an annoyed eye roll. She turned her back on her daughter and headed into the pew toward her seat. However Nancy's father, Bill, took his daughter in his arms for a loving hug and whispered something for only her to hear.

Nancy's groom took her hand and together they stepped onto the Double Wedding Ring masterpiece that her friends had further surprised her with. Marge stepped forward as did Michael's son, Nick, the best man.

This was one of the most beautiful weddings that Nedra had ever seen.

At the reception, the cool of the floor radiated through Nedra's tired bare feet within moments of slipping off her stunningly gorgeous Christian Louboutin Cinderella shoes under cover of the table. Blessedly, the evening was nearing an end and she was finally able to have some alone time with her plus-one guest, Nate. Exhausted from a long day— make that week— of wedding activities she leaned into his shoulder. Nate lifted his arm around her neck and drew her in for a reassuring embrace.

"You girls pulled off the perfect surprise wedding for Nancy," Nate said. "I'm beyond proud of all of you."

"Thanks," Nedra said. "It was a lot of fun but a ton of work. I'm soooo glad it's over with."

Nate whispered into Nedra's hair, "Your wedding obligation is complete and tomorrow you can start full-time on your dream."

"I may need a few days to recuperate from pulling off this 'simple' wedding." Nedra made air quotes when she said the word *simple*. "But I'm definitely looking forward to being consumed with writing."

"I know you've done a lot of the preliminary work with organizing your research and I'm sure this is an unfair question to ask...but do you feel you can finish the novel in the six months leave of absence from work?"

"I'm hopeful, but never having written a novel before, well, I'm not really sure."

"So tell me, wedding planner extraordinaire and most excellent love of my life, is there anything I can do to support your transition to famous author?" Nate caressed her cheek. "Like make some bookshelves, move a heavy desk into some special spot with perfect lighting, or maybe give you a hand massage after a long day of typing on your laptop? How about if I bring you dinner and we eat in front of a roaring fire every night?"

"Actually some of that sounds darn good. I'll take a regular hand massage and dinner by the fireplace."

"You've got it. I'm at your beck and call, my lady."

Nedra sat up straight and looked directly at Nate. "I've got an even better idea," Nedra said. Nate's eyes sparked to life. He was the kind of person who was happiest when he was helping someone else, and Nedra almost felt guilty for what she was about to say. "Well..." She dragged out the word in a singsong fashion. "Why don't you write the book for me?"

Nate's head snapped back as he laughed. "Woman, are you crazy? Having me write a book is sure as heck not the way to become a bestselling author."

"Aw, come on. Be my hero." Nedra snuggled back into Nate's arms and sighed. "I've waited a lifetime to do this and now that the opportunity is here...well, I've gotta be honest Nate. I'm scared to death."

"I would say that under the circumstances, that's a perfectly natural feeling to have." As he massaging her neck ever so gently, his deep voice rolled over her like hot fudge on ice cream—warm liquid comfort. "You can do it, Ned. I know you can. You're the smartest and strongest woman I know. Don't start out with fear or it will take control and eat you up."

"But what if it's horrible..."

"Shhh." Nate placed his index finger over her lips. "Then you'll try again. You can do it. You'll figure it out."

The overhead lights flashed and the DJ said, "Ladies and gentleman last dance. Grab your sweetheart and make some memories before we all turn into pumpkins."

Nate stood. "Come on, gorgeous, dance with me."

Nedra walked barefooted to the dance area on the arm of her prince, leaving her Cinderella shoes under the table.

The stillness of the Mayflower Quilters Retreat was beginning to come alive with an occasional sound. Nedra could hear a shower running next door to the room she was sharing with Helen, and the aroma of fresh coffee wafted down the hallway and crept into their room.

Rolling over, Nedra opened her eyes. Helen was looking back at her from the other bed.

"Did this really happen?" Helen's voice was thick with sleep. "Is Bridalmania finally over?"

"I think so," Nedra said, "unless we dreamed it away."

"I feel like I've been run over by a sleigh and dragged through miles of snow. If another one of us gets married, I have two words." Helen repositioned herself on her back and looked at the ceiling. "Las Vegas."

"Seriously?" Nedra said. "You mean you aren't dying to do this all over again?"

"Nope. I've got it all planned out. We'll take up a collection. The bride and groom will fly to Vegas where they get married by a look-alike Elvis as a videographer captures the special moment for us to watch on live feed back home. We'll all sit around the television eating tons of food and celebrating long-distance with the bride and groom." Helen swiveled her head to see Nedra. "What do you think of that?"

"Stunningly brilliant," Nedra said. "I'll gladly donate a hundred bucks to that cause…maybe even two hundred."

A knock sounded on their door, but before either of them could say anything Rosa burst into the room.

"I'm glad you guys are awake." She stood over Nedra and made an urgent 'sit up' motion with her hands. Nedra obliged and leaned against the wall. Rosa bounced onto the mattress and positioned herself next to Nedra.

"You aren't going to believe this," Rosa said in a loud

whisper.

"Spill," Helen said as she also sat up.

"Lettie is attracted to that guy who drove the sleigh." Rosa sat tall, puffing out her chest after delivering this newsy tidbit.

Nedra looked to Helen and they rolled their eyes in unison.

"What?" Rosa asked. "Don't tell me you both knew about this!"

"We watched it unfold in living color yesterday," Helen answered.

"She was practically drooling," Nedra said and pulled her knees under her chin. "At one point I suggested she might want to close her gaping mouth and stop panting. Why do you think I suggested she sit up in the driver's seat with him?"

"I *never* saw a thing." Rosa faked shock by placing a splayed hand on her chest. "I must have been busy with wedding stuff or something."

"Yeah, I'm sure you were," Nedra said, sarcasm filling her voice.

"How did you finally find out?" Helen asked.

"She told me this morning she thought he was hot," Rosa said. "She wanted to know if I knew anything about him."

"Well, do you?" Nedra said.

Rosa shrugged her shoulders. "Not a blessed thing. It's like he fell from the sky."

"Yeah, with a big-ass horse," Helen said.

"I must say he *was* rather captivating," Nedra added. "Not to mention easy on the eyes, too."

Another knock was followed by Lettie entering the room. "I see Ms. Paul Revere has already started her gossip rounds this morning." She scooched onto Helen's bed and sat cross-legged. "My ears were burning while I was on the toilet."

"So what are you going to do about it?" Rosa's enthusiasm made Nedra smirk. It was always interesting to watch someone on the Rosa Mitchell Hot Seat.

"Well, let's see...how should I put it?" Lettie placed a finger to her lips and looked heavenward as if in deep thought. "Oh yeah...zip, zilch, nada."

"Oh, come on," Rosa wailed and spread her hands in front of her in exasperation. "An opportunity like this doesn't come along very often. You gotta work it, girl. You gotta make it happen."

"Who do you think you are...Dr. Phil? And exactly what opportunity are you talking about?" Lettie's lips formed a tight seam that dipped down at the corners.

"Isn't it obvious? He's a good-looking guy who appears to be available, and you're a single woman in need of a boyfriend. It's simple math, Lettie. You know, two plus two."

Lettie stood and Nedra could tell she was peeved. As usual, Rosa had gone too far. "I prefer chemistry over math when it comes to a boyfriend AND for your information I'm not in need of a man!" Lettie gestured, arms outstretched and hands flailing in front of her. "My fifteen minutes of romantic infatuation with a hot-looking, horse-owning coachman is over." She sliced her hand through the air to indicate finality and spun on her heel to go.

Rosa reached out to grab her friend's hand before she was able to leave the room. "I'm sorry, Lettie. I'm really sorry. I didn't mean it like that. You know my mouth works before my brain has a chance to filter what I say." She tugged on her friend's hand. "Come on, sit down and let's talk to Ned about what we were discussing in our room."

Lettie flounced back on the bed and said, "Whatever."

Helen reached over and patted her arm.

Nedra felt her eyes go wide. *Oh no. Please God, not me.* Becoming defensive, she reminded everyone, "We've already discussed my relationship with Nate a million times," she said. "And even after a beautiful wedding, we're still not getting married."

Rosa waved a hand in front of her face. "We know that. We want to know…"

Marge and Beth arrived on the scene without knocking.

"We could hear you guys from next door." Marge squeezed next to Lettie, who pushed over to make room on the bed for her. Beth spun the desk chair around and sat on it. "What's going on in here?"

"Well to start with, Rosa has already insulted me," Lettie sniped, "and she's about to start in on Nedra. You're just in time for the next inquisition."

"So what gives? Did we miss anything good?" Beth looked to Rosa, the interrogator of the group, and then Rosa turned to Nedra.

"We were just about to ask what your plans are for your first book." Rosa leaned against the wall, sporting a smug look while encouraging her friend to fill in the blanks.

Relief flooded Nedra — this would be easy. "I've got to be honest, I'm a little apprehensive. I feel like I have a ton of pressure on me to accomplish my lifelong dream in six months or less." She leaned her head against the wall and let out a ragged breath. "Some of my preliminary research is finished and I've worked out a tentative outline. I think I'm in good shape to dive in and actually start writing after I get under control from this wedding."

"What's it about?" Rosa asked. "Am I in it?" She was dead serious.

"Not unless you came over on the Mayflower," Nedra said.

"Oh, cooool," Beth said. "I'm glad you're going that route."

"A good portion of the research was already done when I worked on the article for *Excel*. It seemed like a no-brainer to me," Nedra said.

"How long will it take?" Rosa again.

Bless Marge who came to the rescue. "For the love of God, Rosa, she's only been off work for a week, and most of that time has been spent with wedding preparations. You can't just spit out a book. It takes time."

"We're all excited for you and can't wait to hear details." Rosa smiled, and Nedra was touched by her enthusiasm.

"I've never really worked out of the home before and I don't want to get waylaid by chores," Nedra told her friends. "I want the fallout from this wedding and my girl's Christmas visit behind me so I can start writing with a clean slate. It might take me two or three days to get organized."

"Good idea," Marge said. "Organization is the key to success."

"So true, so true." Nedra stood. "With that in mind I really need to get going. I'd like to get home and accomplish as much as I can today."

"Agreed," said Helen. "I think we all need to decompress after the past week."

"But she never answered my question," Rosa said with a bewildered look to no one special. "How long do we have to wait?"

Nedra puffed her cheeks out in relief as she watched Lettie take Rosa by the arm and say, "Leave it alone, girl. You've already managed to piss off one of us today."

Chapter 5
Lettie

Her beloved vintage Mustang was loaded down with all manner of wedding paraphernalia, from piles of quilts that had been used as decorations to mounds of dirty clothes. Lettie thought that maybe she should have brought her truck instead of her Pony, as she called her treasured car. It had sat outside in the cold and snow at the MQR, but fortunately roared to life when she turned the ignition key this morning. When was the last time she had exposed the Pony to the harsh elements of winter? She couldn't even remember. And the salt on the roads, yikes! *I'll need to get it somewhere to clean the undercarriage so it doesn't corrode. What was I thinking?*

By the time Lettie approached the lane that lead to her farmhouse, thoughts of the past few days had diminished. She looked forward to starting a new year with the creative challenges that new projects bring. Being used to living by herself, she longed for some 'alone time.' She hadn't spent one artistic minute in her studio since the first of December, and decided this would be a good time to complete a tapestry she had started as a commission. It would be helpful to get some money flowing again now that the holidays were over. Her 'cash crop' of scarves had completely sold out from various galleries and high-end boutiques that carried her items. No doubt those checks would take a while to dribble in. Her Etsy store had performed better than she could have hoped; that money was hers as soon as the item sold.

The tapestry order would bring in a pretty penny and Lettie was so darn close to having it finished. *I could have it completed by late tomorrow. Then I want to start on that idea for miniature quilt blocks I've been working on. That's the project I'm* really *looking forward to digging into.*

Turning onto the lane with snow piled high on both sides, the Mustang fishtailed on a patch of ice. The wintry tunnel-like driveway reflected the pearly pink sky. With the deep blue grays of the cold shadowy snow, the scene became an impressionistic image. Lettie stopped her car to soak in the beauty. She squeezed out of the door that was pressed up against a plowed mound of white, and took pictures with her cell phone. This would make a fabulous pallet for a series of work she had in mind. A gallery show was scheduled in Oregon about a year from now and Lettie had been hoping for some fresh inspiration.

She had just gotten it.

The sun raked over the lane from behind her, blasting the moment with broad strokes of pinks and peaches, blues and purple-grays, as tufts of brown corn stalks peeked through the blinding white snow. It was a visual gift…a recipe for a spectacular instant that only she had witnessed. Lettie not only wanted to capture it, she wanted to be part of it. To breathe the cold. To hear the silence. To memorize how it made her *feel* so she could duplicate the emotional experience as much as the colors in her fiber art.

Within a few short minutes the image slowly vanished, reverting back to being nothing more than an average winter day. Lettie mourned its disappearance. Fearful she might have overlooked some mysterious gem from the fleeting winter event, she longed to reach out and grab hold of the short-lived vision, attempting to make it last just a little bit longer. What were the odds that she would have been in the right place at the right time to witness such extraordinary splendor? She had been fortunate indeed.

Lettie drove the remainder of the lane surrounded by the ordinary view of an everyday winter scene. The length of her driveway had been plowed by the same neighbor who had looked after her dog for the days she had been gone from home for the wedding festivities. Her faithful old German shepherd and best buddy, Picasso, must have recognized the sound of the Pony as it crunched over the snowy rocks in the frozen parking area. Exiting his doggy door from the heated garage, tail wagging along with the back half of his body, her pal sauntered over to greet her.

She had really missed this guy over the past few days.

Like always, it took much longer to unload the car than she had planned, and by the time Lettie started the first load of laundry, she had received a text from Marge:

"Somehow I left with one of your quilts. Didn't want you to panic. Pick it up at the retreat any time that's convenient."

Refolding all of the quilts and then organizing them in their rightful places, she was thankful that Marge had alerted her to the missing quilt because, yes...she *would* have panicked.

Lettie took a bag of chili from the freezer to defrost for dinner, and then emptied her suitcase of the trappings of a weekend wedding celebration. The adrenaline rush she had felt over the past several days caught up with her, and Lettie soon realized there wasn't a chance she was going to work in her studio tonight.

Shifting plans, she decided to coax her cherished outdoor dog inside for a few hours of reconnecting. On tap would be a good movie and some wine for her, a few doggie treats for Picasso, and a warm crackling fire for both of them. She would satisfy her creative side and keep her hands busy by working on a knitting project.

A hot well-built coachman was yesterday's fantasy, and he never once entered Lettie's mind.

The two days that followed Lettie's homecoming had been spent working on her tapestry commission. After emailing images of the final piece to the purchaser, she had received approval to ship the item immediately. "Done and done," she said to herself as she pulled away from the post office in Whitney. "Time for some fun."

Six minutes later Lettie was easing her little red truck into the only empty parking space behind the local quilt shop. Plowed snow from the lot had been pushed into three of the parking spaces, rendering them unusable until spring. She was happy to see so many cars—it meant the shop was keeping busy.

Lettie opened the door to the sound of a delicate tinkle from a bell and the unmistakable smell of coffee. Voices and laughter coming from the classroom met her as she entered the Quilter's Closet. *Oh, that's right…it's Sit and Stitch day.* Two women were holding a finished block against several bolts of fabric, moving them back and forth comparing the minutest of details. Another was standing in front of the thread display grasping a handful of various colored spools while searching out additional choices.

"Hi Lettie, it's been a while," Helen joked to her roommate from the wedding weekend as she called out from behind the register. She was bagging a fistful of fat quarters for a Sit and Stitcher. Handing the bag to the customer she said, "Thanks, Heidi. I'll be right here if you decide you can't live without that pattern."

"I've got a feeling you'll see me again before I leave here today," Heidi said, and headed toward the classroom.

"What brings you in, my dear?" Helen walked toward Lettie, stopping on the way to rest a hand on the back of the woman holding the complex block, saying, "You ladies okay here?"

"We're fine, Helen…just being a little indecisive today."

"Take your time," Helen said. She greeted Lettie with a hug and an air kiss. "Surprised to see you here so early."

"Ah, you know me well," Lettie said and explained her trip to the post office. "I'm glad you're here. I want to pick your brain about some ideas I have."

"Sounds interesting. Pick away."

Reaching into a small tote bag, Lettie withdrew some papers. "I have an idea for a quilt...actually a couple of quilts. It's very premature but if this works out the way I envision ...well, I'm thinking of possibly making a pattern book available for sale."

"Now you've really got my attention," Helen said, leaning over the work sheets that were resting on the cutting table.

"In the art world, we'd call this idea a 'series'...a group of finished products that are all related by some means." Lettie shuffled some of the papers until she was pleased with their order. "You know how much I like to work with teeny pieces in my quilts? That will be the common thread along with repetition."

"I'm following you so far," Helen said.

"I've always wanted to combine my two loves of fine art and quilting," Lettie admitted, "but until now I was never fully able to pull it off." Flipping to a drawing on graph paper with a few pieced samples pinned to the corner by a long quilter's straight pin, she said, "It's a little hard to explain. There are many movable options available. I feel the choice of those options will personalize each quilt along with the quilter's experience. Let's start here."

By the time the bell on the door announced Lettie leaving the shop, Sit and Stitch was over, another class had started, and Lettie was the excited owner of a large double-handled bag full of new fabric.

"Thanks again, Helen," Lettie called over her shoulder. "You're the best."

Helen waved goodbye saying, "My pleasure, and keep me updated on your progress. I love the concept."

Helen had offered positive feedback with challenging ideas. Not for the first time Lettie thought how fortunate it was for the local quilting community to have this talented woman employed at the Quilter's Closet…not to mention as a close personal friend.

Eager to be home and inspecting her new purchases, Lettie changed her plans and opted out of stopping at the grocery store for the lone items she had written on a list. *I think a can of tomato soup with grilled cheese sounds just about perfect for tonight. Easy, fast, and I have everything at home. Best of all it means more time for me in the sewing studio.*

Remembering the slick ice at the entrance of her long driveway, Lettie slowed her truck considerably as she approached the road hazard. About a quarter of the way up the lane she noticed headlights bouncing off a snowbank coming from a vehicle that was out of sight around a curve. When this would happen in the summer one of the drivers would simply pull off the gravel, brushing the cornstalks on the passenger side to let the other car pass. But in the winter, with the snow piled high on both sides, it was a different story — someone had to back up.

That's odd. It was a rare occasion to be greeted by another automobile while traveling on this lengthy driveway. The lane only led to her house on one end and the county road on the other. *It must be the UPS truck. That means the yummy new line of yarn I ordered got here double fast.* Putting the truck in reverse and throwing her arm over the back of the passenger seat to turn around so she could back up, Lettie saw a flash of green and froze. The UPS truck was *not* bearing down on her vehicle. The car rounding the bend and racing toward her was her precious Mustang!

Confusion reigned as the scene took a moment to register. *What the…who in the world?* The incident happened so fast, yet at the time Lettie felt as though she was observing this horror show in slow motion. She witnessed her coddled Pony dipping into ruts and potholes and then rearing up to come crashing down on the front tires as the rear slid back and forth. Dread filled Lettie's heart and anger pulsed through her veins. The abused and dented Mustang skidded to a halt about a dozen yards away from her truck. It slipped sideways, kicking up gravel and snow until it was wedged tightly between the two mounds of snow piled high on each side of the lane.

Damaged car doors flew open and three teenage boys burst out, yowling and whooping as though they were having the time of their lives. One by one and limber as white-tailed deer, they hopped on the hood of her beloved vintage car, leapt to the top of the plowed snowbank, and took off howling and laughing—yes, the bastards were laughing as they crisscrossed the adjacent cornfield. Too stunned to speak or move, Lettie watched their shapes grow smaller as they dashed toward the county road. It was all over in a matter of a few horrific minutes.

Logic surfaced. *Cell phone. Call the police.*

Her hands trembled wildly as her attention turned to finding the phone in her purse. But after spotting a movement on the other side of the mangled Mustang she bolted from the truck, cell phone in hand. Disregarding the vehicle that only moments earlier she was overly concerned about, Lettie added her own dents to the hood of the Pony as she scrambled across the dimpled metal to reach the other side.

Picasso, limping and bloody, had followed after the vintage car. When he saw his owner coming for him, he sat in the middle of the road. The aging shepherd waited for his sobbing human to reach him so he could collapse into her loving arms.

Lettie wailed loud and long. "Noooooooooooo!" echoed across the frozen countryside.

Chapter 6
Nedra

The animal clinic was ahead on the right. Nedra spotted Lettie's truck along with Rosa's van in the parking lot. Opening the door to the reception area, she was greeted with a chorus of barking dogs and the distinct odor of numerous animals in a closed up space.

At this point, Nedra didn't know any details of what had transpired with Picasso. Rosa called and breathlessly told her there was a serious problem and that Lettie was alone at the vets with Picasso. "I'm heading over there," Rosa told her. "I hate to bother you on your first week of writing, but if you can spare the time...I think she needs some of us with her."

This, Nedra's first day of writing, had gone okay – not stupendous, but better than she had feared. With a whopping four and a half pages in rough draft form, she felt semiconfident about what she had accomplished. But she also experienced a reality check about the length of time it took to write a book. *At this rate I might have to lengthen my leave of absence.*

"I'm here for Lettie and Picasso Peabody," she told the receptionist.

The woman, whose name tag said 'Judy', stood up from behind the desk. "Follow me." They walked down a long corridor. Swiveling her head so Nedra could hear over the barking dogs and general confusion of a veterinary clinic, Judy said, "Poor Picasso. He's really had a rough day. We've all got our fingers crossed for him. He's such a good boy. I'd hate to see him not make it. Doctor Beryl's the best...if anyone can help him, she can."

So it is *serious. It would devastate Lettie if her cherished shepherd didn't make it.*

Judy opened a door with a sign that read 'Conference Room' and Nedra entered. Lettie sat on an armchair and Rosa perched on the edge of a sofa next to her. The two friends were holding hands. Lettie's eyes were bloodshot and swollen; tears ran freely down her puffy face.

She looks awful.

Lettie rose with arms outstretched. "Oh, Nedra." Hugging, Lettie sobbed into her friend's strong embrace. "They hurt him so bad and I wasn't there to protect him. Why couldn't they just take the damn car and leave Picasso alone?"

More sobbing and more questions emerged, giving Nedra an unfocused snapshot of what must have happened.

"Why? What makes someone so warped that they would hurt an old harmless dog?" Lettie held her at arm's length and her voice became forceful. "I can tell you one thing, if they ever catch those punks you'll have to get your brother to act as my lawyer because I'll kill those bastards with my two bare hands."

Nedra slipped her arm around Lettie's back and guided her toward the chair. "I understand one hundred percent," she said. "Pets are part of the family and Picasso is your baby." After escorting her troubled friend back to the chair, Nedra took a seat next to Rosa on the sofa and said, "If you feel up to it, can you fill me in on what happened?"

It was just shy of two hours later when the vet entered the room. All three women sat side by side on the sofa with Lettie in the middle, gripping each other's hands. Mounds of used tissues littered the coffee table. "He's a fighter," Doctor Beryl said.

"Will he live?" Lettie asked.

Nedra knew this was forefront on her friend's mind. Several times Lettie had chanted a simple prayer just loud enough to be heard. "Please let him live. Please let him live." Clarifying her request at times she added, "Please let him live and not in pain."

"I'm fairly confident he will pull through."

Lettie slumped, dropping her head onto Nedra's shoulder, and Nedra felt her friend's body shudder.

"However," Doc Beryl continued with a hold-on-a-minute voice, "It will take a long time, and I mean a very long time. His right front leg was broken and he also has three broken ribs. My guess is that he was kicked several times causing internal injuries as well as broken bones."

This information triggered Lettie to cry even harder. Nedra placed an arm across her friend pulling her closer, while Rosa rubbed her back.

"We'll obviously be keeping him here for a while. You can call or visit whenever you like to check on his progress. Judy's preparing a thorough report for you and she'll bring it back when it's complete."

"Can I see him?" Lettie asked.

Nedra thought her friend sounded as though she were begging and prayed the doctor would allow the visit for the peace of mind that Lettie so desperately needed.

"Normally we don't allow it at this point. The equipment, wires, and bandages can be upsetting for the human. But in this case," Doc Beryl held out her hand for Lettie's, "this guy looked worse when you brought him in than he does now, so it might do you good to see him resting comfortably. He's heavily sedated so he won't recognize you *or* your voice." She hesitated a beat. "Do you think you can handle it?"

Lettie pressed her lips together and nodded.

"You ladies stay here," the vet said. "We won't be long."

After Lettie had left the room and the door was closed, both women fell back onto the sofa. Rosa blew air out her mouth from puffed up cheeks and said, "I need some wine."

"I'm right there with ya, sister," Nedra said. "One thing's for sure, she shouldn't be alone tonight."

"Yeah," Rosa agreed. "I'll get some pizzas from The Depot and spend the night with her. Maybe we'll tie one on."

"Might be just what she needs," Nedra said.

"I sure as heck know it's what I need." Rosa rubbed her forehead as if she were trying to clear her mind. "If you want to join us you're more than welcome, but I suspect you'd like to get back to working on that best seller."

Nedra smiled. "I really should. After all, it's not going to write itself." She smiled again.

"Lettie's one tough cookie," Rosa said. "She'll want to get back to some kind of routine as soon as possible, but I think I'll see if one of the other girls can drop by tomorrow. I suspect it'll be a good idea to check up on her for a few days."

"I agree. But after what she said, I'm afraid she's also going to want to hunt down those cretins that beat up Picasso and exact justice."

"I only hope that it's justice she's after."

January claims the sunlight swiftly, and by the time Nedra returned home it was necessary to click on the lights in order to see. Settling into her cushy office chair with a hot cup of tea, she lifted the lid of her laptop. The words that had been flowing freely from her fingertips, through the keyboard and onto the screen before Rosa's phone call were now blocked by thoughts of Lettie and Picasso.

Attempting to get back on track, Nedra reread the few pages she had written. She deleted several words and phrases and replaced them with a more refined approach. Back and forth she went between the slightest variations in words— sometimes only to end up back with the original sentence or perhaps adding a new paragraph of information or dialogue. Moving forward through the pages, dissecting her sentences, Nedra was finally faced with a blinking cursor on a white background.

After working on the rewrites, she had successfully

refreshed her thought process and, without even noticing it, the words began to flow again.

Chapter 7
Lettie

With head tilted and cell phone firmly trapped between shoulder and ear, Lettie felt somewhat annoyed by the call. "Where?" she said, a little more gruffly than she normally would.

"My place," Marge answered, and then asked, "What's that horrible noise in the background?"

"A drill. I'm installing a doggy door from the garage to the house for Picasso. Once he gets home, I want him to be able to come inside the house as much as his doggy heart desires."

"Good idea. I imagine he'll appreciate spending more and more time inside during the cold weather." There was a pause and then Marge finally said, "So what do you think? Will you come tonight?"

"I don't really feel like going out." Lettie knew what her friends were doing. They were rallying around her. One of the things at which the Bunco Club was skilled was supporting one of its dice-tossing quilting sisters in need.

Not to be put off, Marge countered with, "Then we'll come to you. A sew will be good for all of us. After the amount of time we've spent on Nancy's wedding, no one has had a chance to put needle to thread since long before Christmas."

Oh, crap! That's all I need is a houseful of people. Yet, knowing that Marge would *never* take no for an answer, Lettie finally caved in—but not before she let out a long annoyed sigh. "What time should I be there?"

"Six thirty. I'm making soup and Phree is bringing bread from Panera," Marge said. "Oh, and Helen is making scones for dessert, so come hungry."

'Aye, aye, Captain' was on the tip of her tongue, but Lettie managed to stifle it. She simply wanted to be left alone by everyone so she could sulk and wallow and be angry with the world over what had happened. As irritated as she was by the interruption of her planned pity party this evening, Lettie knew her friends were simply trying to help. At that reminder, her mood shifted and she gentled her voice. "I guess I could use a little fun in my life right now."

Lettie stewed for a short time after feeling manipulated by Marge. When the doggy door was fully installed and all the tools had been put away, it was almost time for the appointment with the electronic security people. As much as she didn't want to have an alarm system, she needed to be realistic. She lived alone in a farmhouse miles from the nearest person, yet close to an urban area. Her dog had been hurt and her car had been stolen and damaged. In a way she was lucky it hadn't been any worse. Picasso could have been killed. What if she had been home when it happened? Would they have hurt—or maybe even killed her? Lettie had never felt threatened being alone in her own home; even walking to and from her studio in the barn late at night had never fazed her in the least. It only took this one horrifying incident for her mind to rush toward fear and envision the unthinkable.

Those creeps had destroyed her car and nearly ended her dog's precious life, but equally awful they had stolen her sense of security. And for this, Lettie was filled with rage.

Flashing on Rosa's words from a few days ago, she stood in her kitchen and stiffened her spine. "I don't need a man, Rosa Mitchell. I can take care of myself, thank you very much." Lettie pointed to the doggy door as though Rosa were there. Shaking her finger at Picasso's new entrance, she said, "Look at that. I put that sucker in myself. No man was necessary." Jabbing a thumb into her chest she added, "This woman rocks." With hands on hips she continued her rant. "And for your information, Miss Bossy Pants, I'm getting a security system installed today. Again, NO MAN NEEDED! I'm a survivor…a loner…unafraid of anyth…"

Lettie jumped in place when a strong knock sounded at the door. One hand flew to her chest and the other to the knife block on her counter. With pounding heart, darting eyes, and the biggest knife she could grab, she crept toward the front of her house. The knock came again just as she got to a window and saw the ADT truck outside. Releasing a soft *whew* of breath, she stashed the big sharp embarrassing knife under a quilting magazine on the coffee table, and opened the door to two unsuspecting ADT installers with their photo IDs and credentials clearly visible.

It had been a long day and she really *really* didn't want to go anywhere tonight. The thought of leaving home and returning alone in the dark and cold was not her idea of a good time. "And just to set the record straight, Rosa," she spat while pulling away from her home and heading to Marge's house, "by 'alone' I mean that Picasso will not be with me."

Why does her thoughtless comment bother me so much?

Lettie intentionally planned to arrive a little late to the 'rally', as she called it. That way her truck wouldn't be sandwiched into Marge's driveway by other vehicles, thus making an early and swift escape impossible if one were needed. She appreciated their concern. Deep down she knew it was thoughtful and kind, but she simply wanted to be alone and to be left alone. By the time she walked to Marge's front door, she had worked herself into a tizzy about all the questions she'd be faced with.

Take a deep breath. These women aren't to blame for what happened. They're only trying to help you cope by taking some pressure off your day.

"There she is!" called Beth. "We were beginning to think you might not make it."

Lettie smiled politely.

"How are you doing, girlfriend? Grab a bowl and get

yourself some soup," Phree said. "We thought we should all eat first so we don't spill anything on our projects."

Lettie smiled again and nodded, saying, "Good idea." She had to admit the soup smelled fantastic and so did the yeasty warm bread. It occurred to her she hadn't eaten since her morning bowl of oatmeal.

"You've really been through it these past few days," Helen said. "How are you holding up? How's our big guy doing?"

Lettie couldn't be angry with these people for very long. It made no sense. They loved her and were simply trying their best to comfort her. The least she could do was appreciate their kindness. At that point, she'd more than likely find the evening to be healing. "All I can say is that at the moment, I'm hanging in there," she offered by way of explanation. "As far as Picasso goes..." Lettie paused for courage as she didn't want to start crying. "I guess you could say the same for him. He's being brave and trying his best to stay with us." Lettie felt tears but fought them into submission.

Rosa placed a hand on Lettie's and squeezed. "How was he today when you saw him?"

"Poor guy. He's still in a lot of pain and pretty drugged up." But Lettie smiled when she added, "He recognized me when he saw me and his tail thumped strong and firm, just like his old self. It gave me hope."

"That's a great sign!" Marge said. "I'm happy for both of you."

"Sorry that we all couldn't have been at the vets when you needed us," Sunnie said.

Rosa's tone was somewhat defensive. "I didn't have time to call everyone. Besides if we were all there it could have been too much for..." she let the sentence trail off.

"No problem, it worked out fine. I'm glad Rosa and Nedra were there. I wasn't holding it together very well and they helped keep me grounded. I easily could have lost it, especially if Picasso didn't make it." Lettie shook her head and again moisture crept into her already sad eyes.

"What are the police saying about the jerks that did this?" Beth asked.

After an exasperated exhale, Lettie said, "The sad truth is that there is almost no way of learning who they are. There were no finger prints; they probably wore winter gloves because of the cold. I never got a good look at any of them and once I saw Picasso, well…they were no longer my priority."

"That's understandable," Phree said.

"I only know that there were three of them and I'm fairly sure they were all teenaged boys. I'm stumped as to why they would go all the way out to my farm to steal a car. It doesn't make sense."

"It *is* one hell of a cool car," Rosa said.

With hands outstretched, Lettie shrugged her shoulders and said, "But how in the world did they even know there was an old Mustang in my garage?"

Heads shook as no one had an answer to her question.

Nedra must have decided it was time for a subject change. "So you had the security system installed today. How'd that go?"

"Quite well. After what happened I'm pretty creeped out. Apparently, I'm afraid of my own shadow." Lettie filled them in on her knife-wielding incident, and by the time she was finished everyone was laughing, including Lettie.

"The whole house and garage is secure, and so is the studio. I've even got a special button on the fob-thingy they gave me for when I walk to or from the studio. No more knives for me," Lettie said.

"Sounds like you've got things under control," Beth said. "What about the car?"

"That's another problem…and a big one," Lettie said.

As the women finished their soup, Marge had been

clearing the table to make room for stitching projects. One by one they each claimed a tote bag or basket from the heap of belongings on the floor. A variety of handwork was revealed: from Helen's paper piecing hexagons, to Phree's wool penny rug, to the hand quilting Marge was doing for her future grandbaby, to Lettie starting a new scarf for next Christmas season's inventory.

"So what's going to happen with it?" Sunnie asked. "Phree told me that you had the Mustang towed back to your garage after the police were finished with the report."

"Yeah, it makes me sick every time I see it sitting there dented all over. I'm going to have to do something soon or it will drive me crazy." Lettie added a bead to her next stitch. "I got a few names from the police and the insurance company. One name was on both lists—McKinnon's Auto Body, down in Peotone—so I think I'll start there. Anybody hear of him?"

Heads shook and Rosa said, "I leave that kind of stuff up to Terry."

"He's supposed to be the best mechanic around for vintage cars. I'm going to call his shop tomorrow and get the ball rolling."

"Hey, has anyone heard from Nancy?" Nedra asked.

Head bent over a small divided bin, Phree scrutinized spools of Valdani thread looking for the perfect color. She pulled out two of the jewel-like balls and examined them closer. "Beyond the photos she posted on Facebook from their nice warm beach in Hawaii, nothing that I know of."

"I warned her off texting us or calling," Rosa said. "She's on her honeymoon, for God's sake. She can tell us all about it when she gets back."

Lettie was happy the focus had shifted and she was no longer the center of everyone's questions and comments. She would make sure the conversation kept away from her. They had hit the high points about her state of affairs and it actually felt good to share her thoughts and concerns. In the long run, she was glad she had joined her friends tonight. "So Nedra," she said, "how do you like not having to leave the house every day for work?"

"I wondered about that, too," Helen said.

"At first I didn't like it. It felt like I had too much freedom and I couldn't rein it in. But it didn't take long for me to figure out that discipline would be the key to staying on track. It's made the last few days more productive."

Talk flowed easily between the women as it always did.

Marge updated the group about Val's latest doctor appointment, sharing a sonogram of the baby.

Rosa proudly mentioned that with the help of a tutor, Ricky had caught up in school and was on track to graduate with his class.

Beth's dad, George Munro, and his girlfriend, Daisy, were talking about getting engaged but not married. "Go figure," said Beth. "I can't keep up with what they're thinking."

Helen carried a plate with two varieties of her much loved scones to the table, resting it in the middle of the women like an offering of gold to a king. "Eat up, ladies. I don't intend to take any of these delicacies home with me. My waistline couldn't take it."

When it was time to leave, Lettie felt sad the evening was over. Even though she had fought getting together with her friends, in the end she was glad she had made the effort. This was exactly what she needed—some good old fashioned girl time.

Chapter 8
Nedra

With a splash of garnet colored liquid, Nate topped off Nedra's wineglass.

"The food was spectacular. You're quite the chef," Nedra said. "It was just what I needed...the opportunity to keep writing and not think about what to cook for dinner." Raising her wineglass toward her very own sexy sommelier, she added, "Many thanks."

Nate had brought takeout pasta from a local restaurant, complete with garlic bread, perfectly paired wine, and an Italian salad. An oversize slice of Tiramisu waited in a box to be shared later.

"Anyway, as I was saying, the point is that I very much like the story I'm working on. I personally find it fascinating, but I think it's going to be too big of a snooze for most people. No matter what I do, it reads like a textbook." She took a sip of wine. "I've written factual accounts for so many years that I'm not sure I can even write fiction at this point."

"It seems like historical fiction would be a perfect genre for you...factual but at the same time with made-up elements." Nate drummed his fingers on the arm of the sofa. "So the challenge you face is to make it more interesting."

"I've thought of everything...and yes, I know that 'everything' is a broad brush, but honestly, Nate, I'm stumped. How do I get readers to be invested in these women from almost 400 years ago?"

Both Nedra and Nate rested their stockinged feet on the coffee table.

Nate said, "I admit to knowing nothing about writing..."

"Not true," Nedra said. "You're an avid reader, so trust me when I say that you know a lot more about writing than you think." She waved a hand in front of her face. "Go ahead with your thoughts. Sorry for interrupting."

"It seems like I always hear 'write what you know.' So what is it you know inside and out...what's your point, or points of view that would make this story uniquely yours?"

Nedra pondered this for only a moment. "Well, quilting for sure and my friends for another. This wouldn't apply in 1620, but my communication skills with the Internet."

"There you go. Bring in quilting, sewing clothes, and maybe even the mind numbing task of mending. Needle and thread is a sisterhood like no other. Carry over the power of your friendship with your own friends to the lonely and scared women you're writing about. Have a conflict, like someone is hard to get along with or judgmental of the others or something like that." Nate gave her the big Nate-smile that Nedra loved so much. "And then have them all become Facebook and Twitter friends with the Native Americans."

"You goof!" Nedra slapped him on the shoulder. "Seriously, those are all good ideas...except the last one of course. I could easily see the desire for the women to bond over sewing, but I wonder if they ever had time for anything other than work and more work from dawn till dusk."

"But the point is that, as a writer, *you* have the power to make it whatever you want as long as it's believable. Make sure the reader sees how difficult yet precious it was for the ladies to have an occasional get together, and how desperately they needed contact with other women. You may have to keep reminding yourself about the *fiction* part of historical fiction."

"That's going to be difficult for me for sure." Nedra lowered her feet from the coffee table and stood. "Are you ready to share a yummy slice of cake yet?" She picked up the empty wine bottle along with the equally empty wineglasses.

"Sounds perfect," Nate said. He piled together plates

and forks to carry to the kitchen as he walked behind the love of his life.

"Coffee or tea?" Nedra called over her shoulder.

"Either is fine. Surprise me."

"Is that my cell phone ringing or yours?" Nedra asked? "I hear it, but I can't remember where I left mine."

They both set the used items from dinner on the kitchen table and zigzagged through the main floor following the chiming sound of the missing cell phone.

"I think it's coming from your purse," Nate said.

Nedra couldn't think who it might possibly be. She had spoken with both of her daughters earlier in the day, and had just seen the Bunco girls last night. Brian? …Maybe Brian. Tapping the screen without looking at the number ID, she said, "Hello?"

Someone was sniffling and in a shaky voice said, "Nedra?"

"Yes. Who is this?"

"It's Kathy, from work."

"Kathy? What's wrong?" Fear dropped like a rock into Nedra's stomach and the room shrunk around her as though she had blinders on her eyes.

"It's Don." Kathy sobbed. "He's had a heart attack."

Don was not only Nedra's boss and mentor, but the editor-in-chief for *Excel* magazine. They had known each other and worked together for more years than Nedra could count. "Is he okay? What hospital is he in?"

"Oh, Nedra." There was more crying and then Kathy keened loud and long, "Don's dead."

Strong arms encircled her as stifled sobs became louder.

"Let it out, sweetheart," Nate said. "I'm right here."

By the time Nedra could speak again she was seated on the sofa with one of Nate's arms resting across her back. A mountain of tissue had been used to catch a torrent of tears that threatened never to stop. "I...I...I just can't believe it," she said over and over, as though repeating it would somehow make the horror convincing.

Nate let her talk, as he spoke soft encouragement.

"I mean...he wasn't that old. I wonder what in the world happened." And then she thought of Sheila. "Oh, God, his poor wife and kids."

The more Nedra spoke, the more the fog around her cleared and the quicker her crying turned to sniffles. "You probably heard me tell Kathy that I'd go into work tomorrow to see if I can help in any way. They're going to be stunned and floundering at *Excel*. I really feel like it's important that I'm with my work family. It's so darn sad to think that Don will never be at the helm of the magazine again. He'll never walk through the door...never give out another assignment. And I feel so damn guilty that I haven't been there for the past few weeks."

"Now that has nothing to do with this and you know it. Don't even go there, honey."

Through swollen and bloodshot eyes she regarded Nate...handsome, patient Nate. "You're right. I'm sorry. I guess I lost it for a while."

"That's alright. I understand." He smoothed a hand over her hair.

Scrunching up the damp tissues in her hands into a tight wad, she said, "Don had such a huge influence on my career. He believed in me even when I didn't believe in myself. He gave me opportunities that I never would have dreamed possible."

"Sounds like a great guy, Ned," Nate said. "I know you two built one heck of a strong relationship over the years."

"This is going to leave a giant hole in my life." Then Nedra spoke in a quiet, sad voice. "I don't know what I'll do without his constant influence and support. Over the past several years we even became each other's confidant."

And there it was.

In those first shocking minutes after hearing the news of his premature passing, Nedra hadn't yet thought about the promise she had made to her boss and friend. She actually hadn't thought about it for many years. Don's secret was now her burden, but what she swore to carry out in his name would most surely destroy his wife.

Not wanting to be alone at this sad time, Nedra needed the comfort of another human being. "Can you stay tonight, Nate?"

"Whatever you want, my dear."

"I just don't want to be alone."

With Nate's arms around her and his breathing steady with sleep, Nedra pondered her time at *Excel*. After investigating numerous stories for the past decade, most of the individual details had become foggy. Years later, facts can easily become jumbled with other research, making the truth a gray area. This happened occasionally between the veteran staffers and often their laughter would end with a comment starting: "Remember the time I thought…"

But not this time. Nedra remembered every detail of that story as though it happened yesterday.

It had been six years ago. Wishing to bring awareness to the historical and cultural diversity within the great state of Illinois, Don and Nedra began working on a two-part story about the World Heritage site known as Cahokia Mounds. Extensive research in a small town in Southern Illinois took place over a two-and-a-half-month period. Don made the trip to the mounds while Nedra remained in the Chicago office 'holding down the fort,' as he liked to say. Nedra approved the arrangement since she preferred to be home with her daughters every night while they attended high school. It also gave Nedra the experience of being the go-to person while

Don was away—an excellent opportunity to increase her corporate management and leadership skills.

As a self-proclaimed amateur archaeology geek, Don soon became absorbed with Cahokia. After his first trip to the site, he told his executive assistant, "I knew it existed, but I never took the time to drive the three hundred miles down there. I never thought it would be so incredible. Did you know Cahokia is called North America's first city?"

Nedra, in fact, knew nothing about Cahokia, but didn't think this was the best time to mention that little fact to her animated boss.

"You have to get Brian to look after the girls and go there with me at least once while we're writing the story." He fanned out stacks of books and brochures on the conference desk, yellow sticky notes poking up from between the pages. "The Mississippian Indians who lived there actually had their own version of Stonehenge. The structures, there were five in all, were made from enormous red cedar posts and are called American Woodhenge. Of course the real wood posts no longer exist, but a reconstruction was created for sightseers."

The light in his eyes had never shone so brightly, and his enthusiasm made her want to know more about this historic location. Nedra had a hunch that the two of them were about to write one heck of a story and Chicagoans would be rushing to the heartland of Illinois to see the splendor of Cahokia for themselves.

"I apologize for my rambling enthusiasm," he said. "But I feel as though I just returned from heaven."

"That's okay, Don. I understand. But perhaps *I* need to spearhead an in-depth story on the National Quilt Museum in Paducah, Kentucky." Picking up a book with the image of a stone carving of a bird-like man, she told him, "That's my version of heaven."

Neither of them knew that by the time the Cahokia story went to press, they would both feel as though they had journeyed through hell.

Chapter 9
Lettie

"McKinnon here. How can I help you?"

"Umm, hi there. My car was stolen and taken for a joy ride," Lettie said into her cell phone. Intentionally keeping her description short, she added, "It's badly dented and since it's also leaking fluid of some kind and sounds awful when I start it, I think it will need to be towed. Do you tow or should I arrange to have my car brought to you?"

"No problem, we can tow most any vehicle."

"I'm not sure how all this works." Lettie felt out of her element. Ask her about art or quilting or knitting or any number of things and she could answer with confidence, but cars? She knew nothing more than she respected the reliability of her little red truck, and that she cherished her 1969 Mustang that typically sat dormant in her garage. "Do you need to look at the car first to see if you want to take on the job?"

"I'll do that when I come to tow it," Mr. McKinnon said.

"Oh. Okay." Lettie felt a little foolish. "Sorry, I've never done this before."

"That's alright, I understand. Let me check my schedule."

Lettie heard the loud whine of a power tool in the background while she waited.

"I can't make it till Saturday. Will that work for you...say around three o'clock?"

"That'll be perfect." She recited her address and included some landmarks to help him navigate through the country roads. After tapping the 'end' button on her cell phone, she turned her attention to planning a visit with her favorite four-legged buddy at the animal hospital.

But first she would stop by the MQR to pick up her quilt from the wedding that had accidentally gone home with Marge.

"Sorry I forgot to bring it home last night after I badgered you into coming to my house for a sew," Marge said. "It completely slipped my mind. I guess I should have left it at my house after all."

"And I apologize for not getting here sooner," Lettie told her friend. "I've had a lot on my plate."

Placing a white plastic bag in Lettie's arms, Marge said, "Well, here it is. I still don't know how I ended up with this bundle instead of you."

"Not to worry. Those things happen. It was a crazy exodus leaving here that day."

"Got time for a cuppa?" Marge said. "I heard some news from Ned this morning."

"Sure." Lettie slipped out of her coat and sat in a chair across from Marge's desk. "What's up?"

Marge repeated the sad story about Don's passing as Nedra had told her. She finished with, "There are so many implications to this story, not the least of which is that Nedra and Don were close friends. I also worry that she's going to get sucked back into working at *Excel* before she's had the chance to begin her novel."

"I see what you mean," Lettie said. "Do you think they'd offer her Don's position?"

"I'd be shocked if they didn't. Any time Don was out of the office over the past…oh, I don't know how many years, Nedra has taken over for him." Marge puffed out her chest like a proud parent. "And she's always done a wonderful job, I might add."

"I can't believe this happened in the short time since we

saw her at your house," Lettie said. "But then again, I've had my own mind-blowing split-second experiences this past week to vouch for just how fast life can change."

"As they say, in the blink of an eye," Marge quoted as she poured them each another cup of tea. The two friends consumed several cookies while they chatted about the upcoming week at the MQR.

"It took housekeeping about three and a half days to get everything back in shape after the wedding," Marge said. "I think all traces of Nancy's nuptials have been whisked away and we're beginning to look like a quilting retreat again. Our next group of guests will come aboard ship this Sunday."

"Is this the week that our eldest guest will visit?"

"Yep." Marge pushed the plate of cookies away from herself and toward Lettie. "Irma will turn ninety-eight years old while she's here, if you can believe it. And from what her daughters have told me — who by the way are aged seventy-three and eighty-one — she's as lively as a sixty-year-old."

"I'm definitely going to have to stop by to meet her. We need to make sure she gets on our social media sites," Lettie said, pushing the plate of chocolate chips back toward Marge. "Is she coming alone or with someone?"

"That's the best part, but I'm actually kind of jealous of all of them," Marge said. "There's Irma, her two daughters that I told you about, her fifty-three-year-old granddaughter, and her twenty-nine-year-old great-granddaughter. AND they're all active quilters."

Shaking her head, Lettie said, "Some people have all the luck."

"They requested two suites across from each other. The family chipped in to do this for Irma's birthday. We've got Chef Evelyn making a special birthday cake and Irma's favorite meal for dinner that night." Marge smiled. "Wanna guess what it is?"

"I can't even begin," Lettie said. "Hit me with it."

"Meatloaf with mac and cheese. Her 'kids' informed me," Marge used air quotes when she said kids, "that it's okay for the chef to fill in the rest of the meal with whatever she wants."

Lettie laughed and reached for her coat. "I think you're going to have your hands full next week."

"I think you're right, my friend," Marge said. "Keep us posted about Picasso."

"Will do, and the same with Nedra."

Thinking of getting over to see her buddy at the animal hospital, Lettie was at the bottom step of the retreat when Marge called her name. She turned to see her friend coming toward her with the protective white plastic bag.

"Okay, this is getting ridiculous," Marge said. "If you forget this quilt one more time, I'm just going to keep it for myself!"

Nuzzling forehead to forehead with Picasso, Lettie whispered so only he could hear. "There's my boy. I couldn't love you more, big guy, it would be impossible." Scratching behind his ears and carefully stroking his coat to avoid the broken ribs, stitched lacerations, and shaven areas, she continued to fuss over her four-legged friend.

"What do you think of our favorite senior?" Dr. Beryl asked from behind her. "Do you think he's ready to go home with you today, Mom?" She slipped the stethoscope from around her neck and listened to Picasso's heart and breathing.

"Seriously...home?" Lettie felt tears forming that she couldn't stop. "Yes. Yes!"

"He's making a surprising recovery, and I think all he needs now is some home-style loving."

It took over an hour to prepare paperwork, fill medication, and input a long list of at-home instructions into the system. Lettie made several jaunts to her truck with the miscellaneous detritus associated with a pet's hospital stay.

On the last trip she blasted the heat to make sure the vehicle was warm enough to accommodate a recently hospitalized canine. Limping on his leg cast, Picasso proudly guided Lettie out the door of the animal hospital and, with her help, slowly maneuvered himself into the cab of the little red truck. He clumsily twirled twice on his lame leg until he found a comfortable spot on the passenger seat, where he melted into a relaxed position, snuffled, and closed his eyes.

Lettie took a moment to twist past the steering wheel and encircle her furry best friend with both arms as her tears flowed unchecked.

At last he was coming home.

Chapter 10
Nedra

Only a few weeks had passed since Nedra left work for a six-month leave of absence. The routine of waking at five, getting herself 'office ready,' and then taking the train downtown proved to be less gratifying than she remembered. And then there was the weather to contend with. January in Chicago was brutal anytime of the day but before the sun barely had a chance to rise, it was especially raw. The wind chill off the lake was minus seven degrees this morning and no amount of bundling up could keep the cold from finding chinks in the armor of her layered clothes.

Why didn't I simply tell Kathy that I'd come in later in the day today. There's really no need for me to do this again tomorrow...at least not this early. As Nedra made her way to the *Excel* building, head down to protect against the biting nor'easter blowing off Lake Michigan, she longed for her casual mornings of writing in her jammies at the computer with a hot mug of coffee in hand.

Several *Excel* employees rode the elevator with Nedra, and Don's passing was the only topic being discussed. One of the workers had not yet heard the sad news, and began to quietly cry before they arrived at the thirty-sixth floor. As though in mourning, the doors of the elevator opened slower than normal onto the *Excel* office.

The usually frenetic workplace was quite somber today. Occasionally a phone would ring, but for the most part, the sound of murmuring and sniffles greeted Nedra. No words were needed as she embraced her assistant, Kathy, and their tears mingled over the shocking loss of their beloved boss.

Placing an arm around Kathy's waist, Nedra led her

into Don's office and closed the door. The women sat side by side on an uncomfortable sofa and held hands.

"I used to sit here while I listened to the two of you preparing the day's work schedule or hashing out a conflict of a final draft," Kathy said. "What are we going to do without him, Nedra? He was way too young to have this happen."

"I'm sure corporate will replace him quickly with a competent editor." Nedra tried to assuage Kathy's fears. It was a fair question at a crucial moment.

"It will never be the same. We were like family, the three of us."

That was very true, but Nedra also wondered what kind of transition would be ahead of them and how it would affect her six-month leave away from work. Perhaps the new editor wouldn't honor the agreement. *There's no use to borrow trouble. We've got enough of it on our plate right now.*

"Would you take the position if they offered it to you?"

If she was being honest, she had to admit that very thing had crossed her mind. She knew she could handle the job along with the stress that went with it. She also felt sure that if Don were here, he would recommend her.

"You'd be perfect, Nedra. I intend to tell whoever is in charge that they needn't look any farther for Don's replacement." Kathy started sniffling again and yet more tears escaped her eyes. "You could be Don, I could be you, and Gail could be me. It would work."

"I like the way you think," Nedra said. "But there are a lot of movable parts to this, none of which either of us has any control over."

Six Years Earlier

Another workday without Don. When would he finally finish his research on the Cahokia Mounds? Nedra added an additional manila folder to the growing stack of folders which remained untouched on Don's desk. Midway through tidying the same documents on the credenza that she had tidied yesterday — the papers which hadn't even moved half an inch since then — she stopped what she was doing and wandered over to the floor-to-ceiling window of the corner office.

Thirty-six floors below, the movements were frenetic. People, cars, busses, and trains were all heading somewhere with unmatched urgency. Each individual had their own story to tell...or secret to keep...or a little of both. The waters of Lake Michigan reflected today's bright blue sky and the sun bounced off the waves like millions of sparkling diamonds. The beaches would be packed, the tourists would be thick as flies, and shoppers, diners, and workers would clog the roadways and railways at the end of the day.

Nedra looked at the clock on the bookshelf across from Don's desk. The whirring anniversary clock read 10:48 and she hadn't heard from her boss in two days. *What in the world is going on?*

When this whole project had started around seven weeks ago, Don was as excited as a busload of quilters entering a fabric shop. His enthusiasm made her smile every time they discussed the mysteries of the archaeological site and how they should approach the development of their story.

"Did you know I started out as an archaeology major in college?" he told her the first time they had talked about Cahokia. "I was able to get through two semesters until my parents realized I wasn't going to change to a more sensible major. In other words and in their opinion, a major that would lead to making a decent living."

After experiencing his passion for the subject, Nedra said, "That must have been very difficult for you."

"In truth, probably more difficult for them. I became a twenty-year-old royal pain in the ass. Their bottom line was: They pay the bills so I do what they say. My bottom line was that I would make their life a living hell until they changed their mind—which they didn't. I'm embarrassed to say that I succeeded in my goal quite splendidly." Don shook his head. "Our relationship was rocky. Years went by after graduation where we barely spoke."

"Any regrets?"

"I'm sure all three of us had regrets. Who doesn't when it comes to the parent-child relationship? But this went beyond them forcing me to eat broccoli or not allowing me to ride my bike in the street when I was six." Don exhaled a deep breath. "This was my passion since I was little and they knew it. Dad took me to the Field Museum of Natural History at least twice a month so I could 'get my geek on' as he called it." Waving a hand in front of his face, he said, "Water under the bridge."

But he couldn't leave it alone, and picked at the memory like an itchy scab. "I told myself I'd *never* force my kids to study anything other than what they loved." He smiled. "This is where karma has a way of nipping you in the butt. I now have a first year philosophy major at Southern Illinois and a sophomore in high school who wants to study contemporary dance."

Nedra had to press her lips together to prevent herself from laughing out loud.

"Anyway, that's why the Cahokia story is both important and intriguing to me. I guess I get a bit of a second chance to do something that ignites me."

And ignite him it did.

He calculated that he'd need to visit the actual location two to three times to collect information and experience the site for himself. They set up three separate dates on their working calendar. Since it took nearly five hours to drive to Collinsville, Illinois, where the museum and site were located, each visit was penciled in blocks of four days. Several days were spent arranging interviews with the museum curator and locating local experts. Numerous leads pointed to the same person, a professor who specialized in both the Effigy Mounds National Monument in Iowa and Cahokia. Nedra made the contact through emails and Dr. Kelsey, Ph.D. would be available for an appointment next week.

The ball was rolling and Nedra had to admit that this was such a unique story for *Excel* that she was excited to watch it develop. Don took off for the long drive on Sunday so he could have some time on location before he started interviews Monday afternoon. If all went according to plan, they'd have their on-site interviews and office research finished in two weeks. Another week and a half, maybe two, to write the story and...voila! Cahokia is going to press and Don and Nedra are on to their next story.

The three workdays that Don was away from the office proved to be more demanding than usual for Nedra. Kathy and she worked late hours to assure that they could remain caught up and ready for the next day's work. On Wednesday, Nedra found herself checking the clock regularly. By two o'clock in the afternoon she was more than ready for him to walk into the office at any minute. By five o'clock, she hoped to be going home knowing that her boss was back at his desk where he belonged. She waited until half past five to call him.

"I'm so sorry, Nedra. I was just going to call you."

Yeah, right.

"Professor Kelsey and I have only scratched the surface...no pun intended, and she's agreed to help us out by spending a few more hours with me tomorrow."

She? Nedra's antennae went up. He sounded a bit too chipper but maybe Dr. Kelsey was sitting there with him and Don was acting polite, or maybe.... She was tired and being petty when she said, "How thoughtful of her."

"I know, I know."

Don sounded happy, but Nedra was becoming skeptical. *Quit being snarky. He's simply found someone with whom he can share his geeky passion.*

"We're going to continue our discussion over dinner and then finish up late tomorrow morning. I have mounds of information to bring back." She heard a woman giggle and then Don laughed. "Sorry. Once again, no pun intended."

Mounds...I get it, I get it! Ha ha. "What time will you be back tomorrow?" She sounded abrupt and little suspicious. *Am I jealous?*

"I probably won't make it to the office till some time after five. The traffic should be horrific that time of day as I get closer to the city. Depending on how late it is, I might just head home."

This did not pass the sniff test and Nedra was certain that some form of trouble was brewing. "Have you called Sheila yet?"

"Um...well," he stammered. "I was going to right after I called you."

Nedra did not remind him that *she* had called *him*.

"Okay then. I guess I'll see you Friday morning. Drive carefully." She hung up before he had a chance to say goodbye.

Sitting alone in her office, head resting in her hands, with the staff gone for the day, she was too stunned to move. This was the person who had become her standard for a decent, kind, family man. She never saw a thing in him that would ever point to the type of behavior of which she had been quick to accuse him. Not Don. She had to be mistaken. As his father used to say when he was a boy...Don was just 'getting his geek on' with a knowledgeable professor.

For all Nedra knew, Dr. Kelsey was twenty years older than Don and covered in warts. Nedra laughed at the picture she had created in her mind. A smile remained on her face as she sunk into her office chair, opened her laptop, and Googled a series of words: Professor Rita Kelsey, Ph.D. archaeologist.

It took only a few mouse clicks for Nedra's smile to dissolve into apprehensive concern. Dr. Kelsey was young and not only wart-free but beautiful.

Chapter 11
Lettie

All bets were off.

In Lettie's mind, Picasso could do no wrong. She vowed to grant him whatever he desired from now until eternity. Period.

But the proud shepherd was not the kind of dog to take advantage of the kindness of his human—or was he? Lettie was surprised at how quickly he claimed the sofa in the warm family room as his own. Gone was his insistence of standing guard in the heated garage. She suspected her precious buddy felt a strong association between the beating which he had received and his favorite haunt of hanging around the Mustang's front left tire.

An around-the-clock 'Welcome Home Picasso Fest' was in full force, where continuous hugs and sloppy doggie kisses with tail wagging ensued. Medications were lined up on the counter according to when they should be administered. Specialized dog food was offered at proper intervals and treats with cuddling were abundant. When Picasso slept deeply and peacefully, which was often, Lettie hovered over him. She flip-flopped between serene smiles and occasional crying.

Fury at the cruelty which had so callously been dished out upon her family member was never far from the surface. A fire smoldered inside Lettie to find and punish the subhuman who was responsible for harming Picasso.

It wasn't long before the fine art of extreme mothering had gone too far for her geriatric pal. After wheeling a wagon up to the sofa, she half lifted, half coaxed him onto it, saying, "Time to go out and do your business. Come on, buddy. Let's go."

There was no misunderstanding the look he gave her...*Are you nuts? No way do I need that thing!*

Hobbling to the other end of the couch where a temporary ramp had been created, the big shepherd limped down the incline with confidence and headed for the door. An impatient look over his shoulder told her...*Step on it, Mom. I gotta go!*

She felt pride swelling in her chest and yet more tears forming in her eyes as he took first one and then another tentative step onto the porch. Old enough to know to be careful, but dog enough to want to sniff everything and protect his property, he moved forward without fear.

Lettie crossed her arms against the cold and did what every mother ultimately has to do. She watched him walk off to make his own way.

This afternoon her damaged Mustang would be towed to the body shop but, as the saying goes, the day was still young. Lettie clearly heard the siren song of fabric calling to her, and she could no longer ignore its tempting refrain. The large bag of yard goods she had purchased last week at the Quilter's Closet had sat untouched in her truck for several days. Every time she looked at the parcel, she blamed herself for enjoying a fabric shopping spree while her dog was being beaten and her car stolen. But with Picasso asleep on the sofa, she retrieved the bag from the truck, lifted out several mounds of fabric, and covered her kitchen table with the colorful bounty.

It wasn't long before the carefully chosen colors and patterns invaded the negative thoughts that Lettie had been experiencing. Admiring each individual piece of fabric by smoothing the rectangle under her hand, she restacked fat quarters and yardage into coordinating piles, all the while envisioning finished blocks and quilt tops. Squinting her eyes at each grouping to check for values, she removed any offensive pieces. Back and forth she went, adjusting slight changes, swapping cloth squares in and out of stacks, and giving each pile a final once-over.

A little more than an hour had elapsed when Lettie leaned back in the kitchen chair, folded her arms across her chest, and smiled. Perfection. Now she had to bundle them so any jostling on the way to her sewing studio would not cause unintentional intermingling. A pile of zipper baggies did the trick and into a tote bag they went, along with a bag of doggie treats.

Having learned her lesson from attempting to get Picasso to ride in a wagon, she asked, "You ready for a walk to the studio, big guy?"

'Walk' was all he had to hear, and down the makeshift ramp he wobbled.

The two friends took their time strolling side by side crossing the farmyard to the studio barn in the crisp winter air. Puffs of steam rose as they each breathed out, and gravel crunched under the tires of the wagon. She pulled a cartful of precious fabric and supplies while he limped beside his favorite person. As in past generations, the Peabody farm and all who lived there would survive.

The sewing and fiber art studio had seen no activity in over a week. When Lettie turned the key and nudging the door open with her hip, a closed-up smell rushed out at the two visitors. It wasn't particularly a bad odor, rather a stale scent that within minutes could no longer be detected. Lettie could tell that the short walk had tired Picasso when he immediately went to his doggie bed and plopped down.

"Good boy," she told him.

With eyes already closed, he thumped his tail and then snorted.

It felt good to get back to work and feel her creative juices begin to flow again. Lettie started by unpacking the new fabrics and arranging them on her worktable. She was eager to put her plans into play for a new workshop she wanted to design for the MQR. She chose a stack of fabric, plugged in her iron, and flicked on an Audible book from her tablet. The cadence of the reader, the soft snuffling of her beloved dog, and the steamy aroma of fresh cloth being ironed lulled Lettie into a peaceful frame of mind.

At two forty-five Lettie heard the approach of a diesel engine rumbling toward the farmyard. Fear once again gripped her gut, turning her mouth dry with dread and her heart into a pounding panic. Glancing at Picasso, who stirred at the unfamiliar sound, she reached for the security fob. She hated living like this, terrorized at unusual noises, frightened of her own shadow, and ready to call 911 on the tow truck guy.

The tow truck guy!

She'd been so absorbed in creativity that she forgot McKinnon's Towing was coming for the Mustang this afternoon.

Asking Picasso, "Do you want to come with, sweetie?" Lettie saw raw fear in her pet's eyes. Bending over she calmed him with some soothing words and told him to wait as she flipped on her jacket and pulled on some gloves.

The huge wrecker, painted with blue and red letters that read McKinnon's Towing, reverberated when she walked past it. A tall man was knocking on the door of the farmhouse and a short woman stood next to him. A warning bell went off in Lettie's head. Something looked familiar. Did she know these people? She didn't think so.

"Hi there," she called out. The couple turned around at the same time and Lettie stopped dead in her tracks.

The guy...the hot sleigh driver with the big horse and the Down syndrome woman! This was McKinnon?

"You okay, ma'am?" He started down the porch steps.

Lettie realized she had turned into an immovable statue since they looked toward her. *Move your feet, you idiot! Say something!*

Waving a hand in front of her face, Lettie answered, "I'm fine. We're just a little jumpy around here since...well since my car was stolen and my dog was beaten." *Why did I say we're—he'll think I'm married. So what if he does? He's not here to ask you on a date, silly.*

Her feet finally cooperated by propelling her forward. They all three moved closer to each other and Lettie saw that the woman looked upset. What's-his-name, Lettie couldn't remember, put an arm on the woman's shoulder and spoke softly to her. As they closed the gap...*God, she forgot how gorgeous he was*...she heard him say, "We'll ask her, I promise. Give me a minute."

Cool as a flipping cucumber and maybe just a teeny bit demurely, Lettie held out her hand and said, "I think I know you from somewhere." It wasn't until the words were out of her mouth that she understood she had just used the oldest pick-up line in the world. She felt her face redden.

He smiled and gave the smallest nod of his head when he extended his hand to her. "I think you might be right."

"The wedding..." she said.

"...with the sleigh," he finished.

With eyes gone wide, the woman said, "Robbie, is this the bride? She looks different."

"No, I wasn't the bride." Lettie smiled and felt like saying, *I've never been a damn bride.* But instead she held her tongue and said, "That was my friend Nancy." Holding her hand out to shake, she added, "I don't think I know your name. I'm Lettie."

"I'm Maggie."

Maggie reached out and held Lettie's hand. She didn't let go. Instead, she came to Lettie's side and kept holding hands with her.

Robbie, she now remembered his name was Rob, stammered a bit. "Ummm, Mags, that's not how..."

Lettie stopped him with a headshake, saying, "It's nice

to meet you, Maggie."

Maggie was shorter than Lettie and looked up at her newest friend through thick smudgy glasses. She then looked toward Rob. When nothing happened Maggie said in a loud whisper, "Ask her?"

Lettie saw a yearning on her face but didn't understand what it was about.

Rob raked a hand through his hair. "I guess we'd better get to the question or you're not going to be tolerable."

Lettie stayed quiet as the mystery unfolded.

"My sister here…" he stopped as he grinned and shook his head in a what-else-can-I-do kind of way.

So that's *their relationship — of course!*

Plopping a hand on his sibling's shoulder he started over. "Mags here heard you say that your dog was hurt. She's a bit of an animal whisperer…"

"Oh, Robbie, you always say that." Maggie looked pleased, but her face turned pink.

Flashing through Lettie's mind was the image of a short blonde woman on the day of Nancy's wedding who was standing next to a giant horse while stroking his mane and murmuring to keep him calm.

"Let me finish, sis," Rob said. "Oh what the heck, I might as well get right to the point. Is your dog okay, Ms. Peabody? Maggie would like to talk to him or her."

Lettie spoke directly to Maggie and not through her brother. "My dog's name is Picasso and…"

"Like Pablo?" asked Maggie.

Lettie shot a surprised glance at Rob who was smiling like a proud brother. "We like art," he said.

Lettie hesitated. "So do I."

"Tell me more about Pablo," Maggie said.

Lettie stifled a smile. *Pablo…how cute.* "Would you like to see him?"

"Oh, yes!"

"He's in my studio. Walk with me and I'll tell you what happened on the way." Still holding gloved hands the two women talked as they walked, followed closely by Rob.

Maggie squatted several feet away from Picasso and began to quietly chat with him.

While the dog had never been aggressive and usually loved meeting new people, Lettie kept a close watch. She was uncertain if his recent experience might have tainted his approach to humans. But after a few sound tail thumps with Maggie stretching out a nonthreatening hand, it wasn't long before the animal whisperer was sitting cross-legged next to the plaid doggie bed.

This woman really knows what she's doing.

Rob's head swiveled from side to side and then up and down as he admired the inside of the studio barn. "This is an amazing space," he told her. "You weren't kidding when you said you like art."

Lettie nodded. "I guess you could say it's my life."

Gesturing to a cozy sitting area, she invited Rob to have a seat. There was a red and white retro 1950s table surrounded by mismatched kitchen chairs, a ratty but comfortable sofa, and two matching wingback chairs from the local thrift store which Lettie had reupholstered with quilt blocks. An improvised kitchenette rounded out the comforts of the space. "I call this my 'thoughtful place' after Winnie the Pooh's thoughtful place. It gives me a spot to decompress and regroup after working for hours." Standing next to an electric tea kettle, she asked, "Would you like a cup of tea?"

"Tea sounds perfect, thanks." Rob hesitated a beat as his eyes bounced off several of the large oak looms, a number of spinning wheels, row upon row of yarns, threads, and fabrics, and a quilting center complete with two sewing machines and a serger. "I must say this is *very* impressive." Turning to her, he asked, "Fiber artist?"

Lettie laughed softly. "Ha, what was you first clue?"

"At some point I'd like a tour if you're comfortable with that."

"I'd be happy to." *When was the last time a man was interested in my fiber arts? Umm, like never!* "Your sister looks to be good medicine for my recuperating pup." Lettie prepared the teapot with several bags. "Poor guy. He's really been through it."

"I overheard what you told Mags on our walk to the barn…um, studio…"

Smiling, Lettie said, "Either is fine."

"I have a problem wrapping my head around the fact that people could take pleasure in hurting a defenseless innocent. I'm sorry that happened to him."

Lettie thought his use of the words 'defenseless innocent' probably included both the four-legged and the two-legged variety. "Thank you. I'm still sick over it." The kettle whistled and she poured boiling water into the decorative tea pot and covered it with a quilted cozy. "For a few short moments after seeing my Mustang crumpled and damaged, I didn't think I could feel any angrier. That was until he," Lettie nodded toward Picasso, "limped down the lane after my car." She shook her head. "It broke my heart."

"As much as some of us love our vintage cars, myself included, they are after all just things…not nearly as important as a loved one."

It had been a long time since she had held a meaningful conversation with a man, but this guy was too good to be true. She decided it was time to be polite. "I don't want to sound rude, but if you need to pick up the Mustang and get going, I completely understand."

"No. We're fine. As long as you're okay with us barging in, that is. You and your 'Stang are last on our docket today." He reached for the teapot and topped off Lettie's mug, then his own. "Besides, Mags would kill me if I told her we had to leave now. And one thing I don't want to do is piss off my sister."

"Tell me about her. Who's the oldest?"

Rob leaned back in the wingback chair, crossing an ankle over the other knee and said, "I'm the big brother by a whopping twelve minutes. We're twins."

"No way!" Lettie was mortified when she realized that in addition to her comment, her eyebrows had involuntarily shot up and her mouth gaped open. "I...I'm sorry. I...I shouldn't have reacted that way. But...well...really? Seriously?" At this moment she was sure she'd never see this man again. She wouldn't be surprised if he jumped up, grabbed his sister and left Lettie and her Mustang to rot in hell. He was obviously protective of his sister and she had just acted extremely socially inappropriate.

Instead Rob laughed. "Don't worry, Lettie, it happens every time we tell the story. Trust me, there's no simple way to spring the facts of our relationship on someone."

It was with perfect timing that Maggie McKinnon walked Picasso to the 'thoughtful place.' With a helping hand from Rob, Picasso was boosted onto the furniture where both Maggie and the dog ended up next to Lettie on the sofa. The dog's snout rested in his human's lap as she stroked his soft head.

"What did he tell you?" Rob asked.

For the second time in a matter of minutes, Lettie felt her eyebrows lift skyward.

With short sentences and the thickness of her tongue, Maggie told Lettie what Picasso was feeling.

Chapter 12
Nedra

The idea of being considered for Don's position at *Excel* made Nedra feel both excited and guilty. If Kathy was correct and corporate was seriously considering offering the editor-in-chief slot to her, she would happily accept. She could end up being one of the most powerful African American women in Chicago—maybe even the country. Young women of any color could look up to her and aspire to be like her.

Nedra's big head deflated when she thought of the reason she might receive the coveted promotion. Don was gone—never to walk into the office again. Never to praise her. Never to help her with the many questions with which she would undoubtedly come face to face if she was offered his position. His friendship and advice would be missed.

It was a mess…a sad, confusing, and emotional mess.

And then there was the leave of absence from *Excel* and her novel. She'd only been working on it for a couple of days, but already felt anxious and uncertain of the outcome. She admittedly didn't like the direction her story was going and doubted there would be many readers clamoring to own a copy. Perhaps staying at *Excel* was for the best. At least she knew she was good at what she did and would have a team of reliable people on her side.

If it was possible to be even more selfish, she was happy it was Saturday. She had the weekend to prepare for the interview. Corporate wanted this wrapped up quickly. There would be no wake or funeral to attend for her much loved boss—Don was to be cremated and his wife would hold a memorial service in a month or two.

Once again, Don's secret gripped her—causing fear,

embarrassment, and guilt to surface. And once again, she told herself there was no way his wife could ever find out. They had been meticulous with their planning.

She needed some professional input and having a lawyer for a sibling came in quite convenient at times. Nedra texted her brother, Brian, and a volley of messages went back and forth between them.

> *Hey Bro, wanna do lunch?*
> *You buying?*
> *No, you are*
> *Oh really? Where we going*
> *Your call since your buying*

Nedra could imagine Brian's booming laugh when he read that one.

> *The Cottage. Can you be there at 1?*
> *See you then. Try not to be late*

With almost three hours to kill before she met her brother, Nedra headed to her home office with a cup of coffee. She'd spend some time working on her writing or novel or whatever it was supposed to be. But after entering the tiny spare room turned office on the main floor, Nedra looked at her laptop and stopped in her tracks. She simply wasn't feeling it today. *It's Saturday and I have an interview for a new position on Monday. The consensus at work is that I'm a shoo-in for the job.* This whole novel thing could be a moot point by next week. She turned around, walked out the door, and closed it behind her.

A little time in the sewing room with one of her many UFOs (what quilters call their unfinished objects) would wipe her mind clean of her worries.

Escorted by the hostess to a comfortable chair next to the oversized yet cozy fireplace, Nedra sighed. Brian was late. Brian was always late when they did anything together. *It's a good thing I'm not a paying client of his or I'd be ticked off. And it's also a good thing that he's paying for lunch...that'll teach him.*

Nedra smiled at her pettiness...*sibling rivalry at its finest.*

"White wine, please," she told the server. "The house wine will be fine."

Nestling into the leather chair, she was warmed by the heat from the fire. The temperature had dropped outside. *Maybe I should have insisted Brian bring carryout to my house instead of having to venture out today. Maybe I should have told him to pick me up. Or maybe I should have picked him up...I could have gotten him moving faster that way.*

There was an elephant in the room, or rather in her mind, and Nedra was doing everything she could not to think of it. *How do I tell Brian about Don's secret...or should I tell him anything?* Theoretically speaking, Don had worked through all the pitfalls and everything should go smoothly. She had nothing to worry about and nothing to feel guilty about.

But she did. She did feel guilty.

All these many years later, she still questioned if she had done the right thing. What would she have wanted if she was the wife in this situation? How many times had she gone over the circumstances in her mind only to reach the same conclusion each time? She would never be sure if she had acted nobly or instead enabled her boss to betray his wife.

A beefy hand landed on her shoulder as Brian bent over and pecked her cheek. "Hey, beautiful. How you doing?"

Instant relief flooded her. "Much better now that you're *finally* here." As the older sister, she just *had* to get in that little dig.

"Let's get our table. I'm starved."

One thing could be said about the Barber children: They had good appetites. While Brian was a man of large stature, his sister could eat him under the table and remained fit and thin.

"I hear their handmade burgers are unrivaled in the Chicago area," Nedra said.

"I'm game. Let's get an appetizer or two."

After ordering, Brian said, "How are things at *Excel*? I

still can't believe Don has passed."

"That makes two of us." Nedra swirled the wine in her glass, tipped it to her lips, and drank the last bit. "I've told you that everyone at work has me believing that I'll be asked to fill his position."

"Why do I feel there's a 'but' coming?"

"It's all happening so fast. I think I really want it…and then I'm not so sure."

"You can always quit if you don't like it."

"I suppose that's true."

"So, dear sister of mine, what else is going on?"

"What do you mean?" Nedra fidgeted with her napkin as she looked over his shoulder, avoiding eye contact.

Brian reached across the table and took her hand in one of his enormous paws. "I can read you like a book and something is bothering you. Is it one of my nieces?"

Shaking her head, Nedra said, "No, the girls are fine."

"Then what?"

She looked into his caring eyes. "Can I have attorney-client privileges?"

"Uh oh, sounds serious." He squeezed her hand. "Better than that. You have the brother-loves-his-sister privilege. I will always watch out for you."

Nedra squeezed his hand in return and felt reassured. She was about to unburden herself and tears sprung to her eyes.

"Start at the beginning, darling. Together we'll solve whatever it is."

Nedra did just that. She launched into the tale of Cahokia and Don's changing work habits. Brian listened thoughtfully to every detail she shared and only occasionally asked a question here and there.

"So when I Googled her and found out she was attractive and in her mid-thirties…well, it didn't take a genius to put two and two together. He was spending more and more time away from work traveling back and forth to the mounds in Cahokia. He even took an unnecessary side trip to the Effigy Mounds in Iowa so Rita Kelsey could enlighten him on a few things." Nedra shook her head. "Seriously, Brian, those were his exact words. I'm not precisely sure who enlightened whom about what out in Iowa, but three weeks later he came back to the office with his tail between his legs."

Their server stopped at the table, asking, "Dessert?" She had been mindful of their serious discussion and was kind enough to give them the privacy of a wide berth.

Brian answered. "Two pieces of carrot cake and two cups of coffee." He looked to Nedra, "Or would you rather have tea?"

"Coffee's fine."

"I had never seen him so...so devastated is the only word that comes to mind. He could *not* function. I covered for him the best I could at work. One day I went into his office expecting the usual thousand mile stare. He was sitting at his desk with his head in his hands and he was trembling with sobs."

Brian slowly shook his head. "I feel like I know where this might be going."

"I'm sure you're partially correct...it's pretty obvious. He finally confided in me that he had an affair with the one and only perky Dr. Kelsey. He had been smitten. Ready to leave his wife...his career...his children." Nedra spread her hands in front of her. "Don was being consumed with guilt from two fronts: sick by what he did to his wife and family, and ashamed at what he did with Rita."

Nedra sat back in her chair and exhaled. "This became the turning point for me. He spilled his guts and while it made *him* feel better," she tapped her chest, "*I* now carried his burden."

"Not to sound too callous—but he had an affair. It happens."

Pointing and then shaking a perfectly manicured finger at her brother, she signaled 'just a minute there, buddy' through tightly slit eyes. "I'm a woman and there is no such thing as a wife cavalierly shaking off an affair that her husband took pleasure in. I felt and still feel dirty for my part in this."

"What do you mean your part in this? You're not the one who had the affair with him."

"That's true, but I did help cover it up. I also helped cover up the fact that Dr. Kelsey was pregnant with Don's child."

Brian's cheeks puffed with air and he slowly exhaled. "Okay, you got me. That sucks."

"On one hand I wanted to slap him silly and tell his wife, but what good would that do?" After a moment's pause, she said, "Nothing. It would have done nothing. It probably would have destroyed the woman I was trying to liberate from his lie. I've been over it in my head so many times and I still don't think I should have told Sheila anything. If Don had been involved in multiple affairs, I might have passed on that information to her. But isn't everyone allowed to make mistakes? No one is perfect, right?" After a sigh she bowed her head and said, "I know I sound defensive and conflicted. This has been hard on me for years."

"So did Don break it off after he found out about the pregnancy? How did he fix it so she wouldn't say anything to his wife?"

"Come on Brian, quit being such a chauvinist. *Don* didn't fix anything." She shook her head with attitude. "*Don's* the one who wanted to leave his wife and start a new family. Rita told him buh-bye. She warned him not to contact her. She wanted to raise the child on her own without his presence, help, or money."

"Oh man, you're kidding."

"I think she set him up."

"Whadda you mean?"

"Mid-thirties, ticking biological clock, a relative stranger yet intelligent genes...someone waaay out of her geographic area." She splayed her hands on the table. "I've thought about it for years. It makes sense."

Brian put his fingertips on his temples. "So how in the world did this play out?"

"Don was adamant that he didn't want to be just another sperm donor who was responsible for a child growing up fatherless, but he really didn't have much choice in the matter. And then there was his wife and children to consider. He loved them. He had been a good family man, but he made a stupid, stupid mistake."

"Nedra, this was a lot for you to carry."

"It has been. Don's dead and I need to talk to someone. It's beginning to eat me alive." "You're not thinking of telling Sheila are you?"

"No. Absolutely not. It would prove nothing."

"Then you know you've done the right thing."

"Well there's one more thing."

"Here comes the kicker. I knew it."

"Don put me in charge of a trust fund for Baby Kelsey. You know, in case something should happen to him," Nedra snorted. "Which we were both sure wouldn't happen. He wanted to know that the child would have some money to fall back on in the event that he or she needed it."

"Oh, Nedra. Why didn't you come to me in the beginning? Please tell me this was drawn up with legal counsel."

"Sort of."

"What the heck does that mean?"

"His longtime financial advisor took care of the paperwork. Until I told you today, Joseph Drut is the only other person who knows about the trust."

"Do you have any paper and a pen in that jumbo purse

of yours?"

Nedra unzipped a compartment and shuffled through all manner of necessary debris until finally coming up with the items her brother requested. She handed them over to him.

"I'm shocked you can find anything in there," he said.

"Spoken like a man who needs something but doesn't have the foresight to bring it himself."

"Point taken. But no matter how correct that statement is…I'm not going to carry a purse." He started writing a list on the proffered paper. "Let me look into this on your behalf. Somewhere in there I'm hopeful a lawyer was involved. Get me any contact information on Drut and the name of Don's lawyer if you know it. Also on Rita Kelsey. Let's see what we can find out about her."

"I'll put together some facts as soon as I get home and email them to you."

"And Nedra, next time you're in over your head, come to me first."

"Got it," she said.

While Nedra was slipping on her coat and scarf, Brian pressed his cell phone to his ear and checked for voice mail. She could tell by the look on his face and the way he turned his head toward a quieter corner, that something might be amiss with a client. She waited to say her goodbyes and to thank him for lunch and his help with her dilemma—but she didn't get the chance.

Brian tapped on the phone and hesitated a moment before saying, "It's Phree. She was crying."

Chapter 13
Lettie

Wearing her warm flannel nightgown and soft Dearfoam slippers, Lettie gazed from her kitchen window over a steaming mug of coffee at the neighboring farmer's fields. Sleepy morning eyes along with frost on the windowpane turned the snowy expanse into an Impressionistic type image. Even Monet would be astounded by the play of color.

Turning from the window and facing the reality of her life, Lettie asked aloud, "What the heck happened last night?"

When Maggie had explained that Picasso was sad that he didn't protect her car from those bad people, Lettie had felt tears flood her eyes. Desperately trying not to cry, she had succeeded until Maggie added, "He thinks you are ashamed of him. He's sorry."

That did it.

Lettie's tears fell like Niagara Falls, as her dad used to say. When innocent Maggie gave her a clumsy hug Lettie sobbed even harder, certain she was making a complete fool of herself. If Robert McKinnon hadn't been scared off yet, surely he was now.

Maggie said, "I'm sorry, Miss Lettie, I didn't mean to make you cry. Don't be mad." Lettie took a deep Yoga breath and reined it in.

"Oh, sweetie, I'm not mad...not at all. I'm just being silly and emotional. I feel so bad that my buddy was hurt and that I wasn't there to protect him."

"You two have to talk," Maggie said. Patting her knee she said, "Here, boy."

Lettie wanted to stop her from calling Picasso to them—after all, he needed rest—but she didn't know how to do it without seeming rude to Maggie.

But it was like this little animal whisperer could read her mind. "You baby him too much," Maggie told her in a low voice. "He doesn't like it."

"Oh...I'll have to remember that. Thanks." Lettie finally had the courage to look at Rob, who was attempting not to laugh or smile by pressing his lips tightly together.

Aided by Rob hoisting Picasso onto the sofa, the canine had snuggled in between the two women with his snout on Lettie's lap. "I hear we need to talk," she had said, scratching behind his ears. Three strong tail thumps had signaled that he agreed.

Her first mug of morning coffee was now empty and Lettie rose to pour another. She retrieved a few cold pieces of pizza on a paper plate for breakfast and slipped them into the microwave. The pizza reminded her of how Rob, with a smile and attempting to be polite, had said, "Mags, I think maybe we should get Miss Lettie's Mustang on the wrecker. It's already dark out there and she might have things to do."

With pure goodness on her face and those almond-shaped eyes magnified by her glasses, Maggie looked to Lettie saying, "Do you, Miss Lettie? Do you have things to do?"

At the risk of sounding like a total loser, and with her eyes and face still red and swollen, she answered. "I don't have a blessed thing to do or anywhere to be except right here."

Maggie's head swiveled to look at her brother. "See, Robbie? Lettie said we can stay! And I'm getting hungry."

Rob looked as though he could have crawled under his wrecker. "Maggie, what have I told you about inviting yourself to do things with people? You need to use that filter we talked about."

Hanging her head, she mumbled, "I'm sorry, Miss Lettie."

It was clear the girl was embarrassed and Lettie *had* to

stop thinking of Maggie as a girl. She stood up, nudging Picasso's snoring muzzle off her lap, put her hands on her hips and said, "If you two don't stop calling me *Miss* Lettie I'm going to scream! And believe me I can scream loud. So from now on I'm just plain Lettie, thank you very much." Maggie giggled and Lettie added, "I hope you both like pizza because I'm starved, too."

She hadn't really been starved but Lettie had been in the beginning stages of thinking about dinner.

Even now, in the light of the next day, she didn't know what made her do such a bold thing as invite them to stay for pizza. Maybe it had something to do with Maggie, but Lettie thought it more than likely had something to do with the woman's handsome brother.

They feasted in the studio using paper plates and plastic utensils. Lettie learned from Rob that Maggie was an accomplished crocheter. "She can crochet up a storm," he boasted. "Hats, scarves, blankets, afghans...you name it, she can crochet it."

"I'd love to see some of your work," Lettie told her. "I crochet, too."

Pushing her thick glasses back onto the bridge of her nose and leaving a greasy fingerprint, Maggie said, "I don't know fancy stitches. I do plain things."

"Nothing wrong with that. Plain keeps you just as warm. Have you ever used fancy yarns?" As a fine artist, *fancy yarns* would not have been a description that Lettie would normally have used. When Maggie shook her head, Lettie added, "I'll make you a package of some fancies that I have. It's always fun to try something new. Would you like that?"

Maggie looked toward Rob with a smile that melted Lettie's heart. She bobbed her head excitedly. *I'm feeling a connection with this person and I've only just met her.*

When their luxury dining experience was over, Lettie brought a baggie of homemade peanut butter cookies out of the fridge for desert and they passed around the bag until it was empty.

That was the nicest meal Lettie had eaten in a long time and it was mostly due to her unexpected guests.

Then came the tour of her studio. Here she learned a little more about Rob…but very little. She learned he liked art but was not an artist himself, and that he loved antiques and the history behind them. He was rather ambiguous when he mentioned that he had studied art somewhere, and Lettie felt as though she shouldn't pry. If for some crazy reason they continued to see each other, she'd find out soon enough.

Rob claimed that he fell back on his natural talent as a car mechanic when it came time to earn a living. He had shared countless hours in the garage with his father working on cars. "I'm nothing more than a glorified grease monkey," he said. "And the *glorified* part of my job description exists simply because I specialize in vintage cars."

Again, Lettie wanted to know more, such as, did he have any regrets with the choices he'd made? She decided this was not the right time for that discussion.

"I guess you could say that we're pretty good antique collectors, aren't we, Mags?" His sister bobbed her head as she focused on trailing a length of 'fancy' yarn that Lettie had given her through her short fingers. "We scrounge flea markets and garage sales for treasures. It's always a thrill to find another gem for our home."

His use of the words *we* and *our* in much of what he said did not get past Lettie. *They're a package deal.* At that moment she hoped she'd see him again, and was more than a little surprised by the way she was feeling.

It had been far too late to attempt to evaluate the Mustang and then maneuver it onto the flatbed of the tow truck, so it was agreed that the McKinnons would come back for it tomorrow. "Let's shoot for two o'clock this time." Rob kicked the ground with the toe of his work boot and sent a piece of gravel skidding a short distance across the parking area. "Would you be up for some company again? Mags and I could bring some grub and maybe play a few rounds of UNO."

Maggie bounced on her toes, fingers steepled as if in prayer. "Yes, yes...Please say yes, Miss Lettie. I love UNO."

How could she resist the two of them? "I'd like nothing better," she had said.

The clock in Lettie's kitchen currently read nine forty-five. She had four hours to whip her home and herself into shape before her two new friends arrived.

The hissy fit she had suffered after Rosa's remarks about 'needing a man' came back to her. *Maybe I don't* need *a man to make me happy...but maybe I could be happy with* this *one.*

Chapter 14
Phree

"Calm down," Marge said. "Brian will be here soon. He was leaving The Cottage so he's not far away. He'll know what to do."

Phree's mother, Sunnie, paced the General Manager's office at the Mayflower Quilters Retreat. Every time she passed by her distressed daughter, she lay a soothing hand on her back.

"They can't do this. I won't let them. It's not fair." Phree keened her pain out of her body and into the room. "I'll protest. They'll never take the MQR away from us."

"I'm sure it won't come to that," Sunnie said. "Slow your breathing or you're going to hyperventilate, honey."

Phree held her head in her hands and moaned. Marge closed the office door, and Sunnie hugged her arms to her chest as she continued pacing.

It was a good thing that it was Saturday and there weren't any guests at the retreat. There were, however, plenty of behind-the-scenes employees working to prepare the MQR for tomorrow, when another week of quilters would arrive.

"He's here," Sunnie said as she passed by the large window. "It looks like Nedra is with him."

The brother held the door open for his sister and they entered the room. Brian went to Phree, saying, "What is it? What's going on?"

Phree handed him a tear-streaked letter from the government. "It's something about that Interstate 80 extension they've been talking about for years."

Brian glanced at the letter and collapsed into a chair. "Oh crap."

That did not make Phree feel safe and her tears started once again.

After reading further, he rested the document in his lap, heaved a long breath from between his lips, and said two of the most dreaded words a landowner could ever hear, "Eminent domain."

Chapter 15
Ricky Mitchell

Ricky had a dilemma.

But since he knew what he was going to do, did that still make it a dilemma? To start with, he was going talk it over with his parents and get their advice. No more secrets.

It had been over a year since Ricky had run away from home. He had been only fourteen years old when he was sexually abused by a stranger. He left home when the adult had threatened to harm his mother. To Ricky it was a lifetime ago.

He was currently in counseling, back on track at school, except socially, and had a good job at the Mayflower Quilters Retreat as Head Schlepper. He had been forgiven and then supported by those he had emotionally hurt. Ricky Mitchell had learned more tough lessons in the last few years than most people experience in a lifetime.

But right is right—he had always known that.

When Ricky went back to high school after his ordeal, gossip swirled around school like a tornado filled with debris. Some of the rumors were true while others were not. The fallout from the gossip gave Ricky a 'hands off' status. Other than two good friends, he was neither teased nor befriended. Ricky didn't really mind as he had matured beyond his age. A few friends, his family, and his work were all that was important to him.

That was why, when he overheard a bully in the locker room mention an 'old school Mustang,' Ricky lingered to hear more. Busying himself by retying his shoes, digging through his backpack, and scrolling down Facebook, it wasn't long before he was sure that Alan Reynolds was responsible for the misery which his godmother was going through.

"It sucks that we didn't get very far in that old 'Stang, but it was sure a sweet ride. Dude, that car can kick ass. I floored it and it took off like a rocket sliding down that skinny-ass road."

The group of tough-guy wannabees laughed.

"I'll tell you, bro, it was worth it to see the look on that bitch's face when we skidded to a stop right in front of her." Alan laughed. "Me and Tommy jumped on the hood and took off. I didn't think Tori would make it over the snowbank, but she climbed that hill like there was a firecracker up her ass." Alan laughed again, closed the locker, and hoisted his backpack on his shoulder. "I'm telling you, that chick is off in the head. She's the one that kicked the shit out of that poor old dog."

The entourage passed Ricky without a notice. He wanted to take the creep down then and there, but he knew he was no match for Alan Reynolds.

Invisible Ricky Mitchell would make him pay another way.

Chapter 16
Lettie

Picasso lifted his head with ears at attention. It took Lettie several more moments before she heard the rumble and then saw the wrecker pull into the farmyard's parking area. "Good boy. Nothing to be afraid of, buddy." She bent to give him an ear scratch. "Our friends are coming back for another visit today." Her baby was acting more like his old self.

Not wanting Rob to think she was eager to see him, Lettie didn't rush to the door. She stepped into the shadows of her living room and watched as the brother and sister exited the big truck for the second time in as many days. Rob brought forth several cloth tote bags and baskets from the expansive cab. Maggie hopped on her toes and accepted a few small parcels that her brother handed her. When he finally looked toward the house, Lettie moved forward and opened the door calling out, "Can I help?"

"No," Rob said. "Thanks though. I'll make another trip."

Hmmm, polite and courteous…a gentleman.

The first one to reach the porch was Maggie and she eagerly handed Lettie a bouquet of fresh flowers, simply saying, "From us."

"They're beautiful, thank you." Lettie buried her nose into the flowers, taking an exaggerated deep breath. "And they smell so pretty, too."

"Robbie told me ladies like to get flowers."

"Well, your brother is right about that." Holding the door open wider, Lettie said, "Come on in, Maggie. Picasso has been waiting for you."

Looking quite dashing under the weight of a number of heavy parcels, Rob lagged a short distance behind his sister.

Holding the door open Lettie said, "Welcome." As he passed by, she closed her eyes at the whiff of sexy smelling cologne, admitting to herself that his was a much nicer smell than the flowers.

Wiping the snow off his shoes on the welcome mat, he told her, "I'll set these here and be right back."

Lettie watched as Maggie sat back on her heels in front of the sofa where Picasso reigned as king. Unmindful of her surroundings, with her winter coat pooled around her knees, she still wore her scarf and hat. Maggie McKinnon stroked the convalescing dog as she quietly spoke with him. *Could she really communicate with animals? It sure seemed like it.* But even if she couldn't, Picasso was delighted with the attention he was receiving from his new friend.

Placing a cardboard box containing a slow cooker along with something that looked like a waffle maker on the floor, Rob said, "I think that'll do it."

"It smells wonderful." Lettie was not simply referring to the aroma of the cooked food as she breathed in Rob's cologne again.

"I hope you're hungry. I think we've got enough food for a dozen people."

"Let me take your coat," Lettie said.

"Mags, I'm going to need some help here," Rob said. "Don't forget we're going to surprise Lettie."

With a kiss to Picasso's head, Maggie joined her brother.

"Let's plug in the Crock Pot and get everything organized in the kitchen. Then we'll get that 'Stang on the wrecker." Rob hoisted the cardboard box and nodded toward two of the cloth tote bags. "Mags, grab those bags and follow me." Smiling at Lettie, he asked, "Which way to the kitchen?"

"Can I help by carrying something?"

"No," said Maggie. "We're surprising you."

"Oh, I see." Lettie stifled a laugh. "In that case, follow

me." More than a little curious about what the secret was that these two had in store for her, Lettie attempted to sniff out what was simmering in the slow cooker. She didn't have a clue.

Maggie made another trip to the stockpile at the front door, but detoured slightly to pat Picasso on the head. Glancing into several of the bags she stood and called out, "I found the fruit salad but I can't remember the other thing."

Rob came to the doorway between the kitchen and the dining room, sleeves rolled up and holding a rubber spatula. "The can of whipped cream."

"Ohhhhh, I remember now. I'm sorry, Robbie."

Lettie lit some candles as she watched Maggie head toward Picasso, where she set down the items from her task and snuggled into the dog's neck. A moment later, Rob appeared in the doorway again. He clearly saw that she had been sidetracked. "Mags, bring me those things and then you can visit with Lettie's dog."

He's a saint…that's all there is to it. What drives their loving relationship? Since Lettie was an only child, she had no idea.

The matchstick scraped across the striker and the scent of sulfur filled Lettie's nose. Skilled in fire making, she soon coaxed the wood loaded in her fireplace into flames. Warmth crackled and radiated from the blaze, invisibly moving across the room and shifting the temperature from chilly to cozy.

Occasional chatter came from the brother and sister team in the kitchen. Lettie sat on the hearth, enjoying the warmth. She wondered where this new friendship was headed, that is if it was headed anywhere. But most of all she wondered if breaking a behavior pattern was possible. Could she break the vow she made to herself over twenty years ago to never get involved with a man again? She rarely thought of the reason for that promise but the sting was always there, leaving it impossible for Lettie to ever allow a man into her life.

Mesmerized by the dancing flames, not to mention a man in her kitchen that was a potential love interest, Lettie wanted to break down her fears and give Rob a fair chance. The only way to do that would be to revisit the ugly truth of her past.

The happiest bride in the world wore white. On the limo ride to the church with her attendants, Lettie imagined Eric smiling as she approached him on her father's arm. Her handsome groom would be waiting at the other end of the church's long aisle. It would be her most perfect day ever.

Until it wasn't.

Looking back, there had been red flags — many of them. But being young and in love can make one foolish, and at the time Lettie considered the warning signs to be nothing that love could not conquer.

While Eric was a conscientious worker who maintained a spotless employment record in management at a downtown firm, he never earned a dollar he didn't quickly part with. "We can save later," he'd say. "Let's have fun while we're both young."

He was generous with his obsessive spending and purchased items for both of them, most of which Lettie didn't want or need. She suspected that he rationalized some of the spending by thinking: If I buy this for my fiancé, I can buy something (usually much more costly) for myself.

Thanks to Eric, the two of them had accumulated a mound of stuff, from watches, to never used gym memberships, to cars, to theater tickets, to expensive restaurant tabs, to gambling excursions with the guys, and on and on it went. Along the way he had amassed a mound of debt.

Her parents began to chime in with warnings, which ultimately led to huge arguments between the three of them, the result being that Lettie stopped sharing her troubles with them.

She would cringe each time Eric visited with a package or said, 'Wait till you see what I bought!' She learned to never say anything to him about his spending because it made him angry.

He's always excited and it makes him so darn happy when he spends money. Maybe I should lighten up like he says and enjoy it while we can. Life is too short.

Months before the wedding, an alarm bell should have sounded when they were out for dinner and his credit card was refused and then another was rejected also. "No big deal. There must be a mistake at the bank," he had said. "Here's cash. I'll contact the company tomorrow and sort it out." He had smiled and continued on with the evening unconcerned as they went to a movie. The incident bothered Lettie much more than it did him.

So with the heart of someone head over heels in love, Lettie would tell herself, "It's okay. He'll change once we're married and he has more responsibilities."

Then there was Maura, better known as his ex-girlfriend. Apparently it never bothered Maura that Eric spent money, especially when she was the recipient of his gifts. And apparently Maura began to miss what Eric had to offer and she didn't mind one bit sharing him with Lettie. Only days before the wedding Maura's conscience must have gotten the best of her, either that or she planned to disrupt the nuptials, when she phoned Lettie with some information.

"I don't understand," Lettie had said. "What do you mean he's been seeing you again? He's marrying me on Saturday."

"Not if I can help it," said the 'other' woman.

Thinking back, Lettie was sickened most by her own naivety. How could she have been so stupid? OF COURSE NOTHING WAS GOING TO CHANGE WHEN THEY GOT MARRIED!

But, she had loved him. And she trusted him when he

said it had been a mistake with Maura. In some way she had tricked him. He cried real tears at the thought of losing his wonderful fiancé, promised to never see Maura again, and begged Lettie to forgive him.

What could she do? Over one hundred people would show up at St. Mary's Church in Whitney on Saturday to see them exchange vows. Her parents had paid for everything. *I can't cancel at the last minute.*

After everything that's happened, he still loves me. It will all work out.

Her reverie was shattered as Maggie called out, "Miss Lettie, it's time for dinner. We're going to surprise you."

"I can't wait," Lettie told her new friend, as Maggie took hold of her hand and led her to the kitchen.

"I fixed the table and made it look pretty. Robbie let me do everything," Maggie said.

As they walked into the room, Rob stood with his arms spread wide. "Welcome to your own kitchen. A very late lunch or early dinner will be served as soon as you two sit down." He bowed from the waist.

"Why thank you, kind sir and kind lady," Lettie answered. "I do believe this might be the most beautiful my old kitchen table has ever looked. Did you hire some fancy designer to make it so pretty?"

"No," Maggie called out. "I did it! 'Member I told you?"

Placing her hands on her cheeks in surprise, Lettie said, "That's right, and you did a very lovely job." The items on the tabletop were a little haphazardly arranged, but Lettie could envision Maggie working to make it special. "It is simply stunning."

Lettie was rewarded when Maggie beamed, and further rewarded when she looked toward Rob, arm around his sister's shoulder, who grinned with pride.

"Let's do it before it gets cold," Rob said. "We have homemade vegetable beef soup, turkey and cheese paninis, and my famous chopped salad. And for dessert..." He nodded towards Maggie.

"Cake without flowers."

Rob laughed. "Also known as flourless cake."

"You two have spoiled me forever," Lettie told her guests, but she was stunned by Rob's answer.

"Get used to it," he told her.

Chapter 17
Nedra

Accessing and posting to the Mayflower Quilters Retreat social media sites from home would be quicker and easier than going to the MQR and getting caught in the middle of the Sunday check-in melee. From what Brian had told her, Phree was near hysteria over the eminent domain notice, and Nedra couldn't blame her. She prayed that her brother could straighten out this nightmare and save the retreat from a disaster.

Since Nedra was in charge of the MQR's social media, Brian had advised her to get the word out as much and as often as possible that the government had targeted a portion of the retreat for the I-80 bypass. The road would run smack-dab through the middle of a peaceful quilting haven. "Make this a call to action," he said. "Attach contact information so your quilter advocates can email, tweet, and Facebook these culprits telling them to leave the Mayflower Quilters Retreat alone. Make sure to run everything past me before you post it so we aren't saying anything that might be libelous. We don't want to add to the problem at hand."

Having worked at her computer since seven this morning, Nedra had created a number of blog posts, tweets, and Facebook status updates which she could rotate throughout the next few days. A public meeting was scheduled to be held on Tuesday evening at the Whitney Town Hall and Nedra intended to keep this story alive and in front of their readers.

She clicked 'Send' at ten forty-five and told her brother to have the missives approved and back to her in an hour. That would give her plenty of time for a shower. She planned to get a text out to all of the women in the Bunco Club so they didn't get their information concerning the retreat through a blog post. Finally, by no later than one o'clock this afternoon, she needed to be preparing for her interview tomorrow at *Excel*.

Only twelve minutes off her self-imposed schedule, Nedra had finished sending the private texts and then gone live with all of her posts. Closing the lid on her laptop, she stretched, and said out loud, "Now to focus on that interview."

And then it began.

Her phone started chiming with notification after notification. Her philosophy was: If someone takes the time to respond to the MQR on social media, I will make sure they are answered personally by me or a retreat staff member. She hadn't considered the possibility of the out-and-out uproar she might cause by going public with the eminent domain story.

Quilters across the country were up in arms! Well, at least with their rotary cutters.

Tweets were being retweeted, Facebook updates remarked on and shared, and blog comments were already numbering in the thirties after being posted for only ten minutes. Adding to that, the group text message to the Bunco Club had also caused a stir among the friends that didn't already know what happened.

How was she ever going to concentrate on tomorrow's interview with all of this drama swirling around her?

By four o'clock, with only her clothes laid out for the next day, she simply had to call in some backup. Marge and Phree were busy working check-in day at the retreat, Nancy was still on her honeymoon, and Nedra had already been working the keyboard all day. That left Rosa, Helen, Lettie, and Beth.

After the initial shock wore off and the group texts finally dwindled to nothing, Nedra was left with three of the women offering help if it was needed. This was the first moment she noticed that there had been no communication with Lettie. Surely if she had seen the shocking news, she would have responded by now.

So the question remained: What in the world was Lettie doing that she hadn't looked at her phone all day?

Chapter 18
Lettie

Curled and sleeping around Picasso on the sofa was an exhausted Maggie McKinnon. On the floor beneath her was a tangle of fancy yarn in a basket, crochet hooks, and a practice swatch with one new crochet stitch Lettie had shown her.

"I'm not sure what she enjoyed the most: being in on a surprise for you, playing UNO, or crocheting with someone," Rob told her. "Thanks for being patient with us. Not a lot of people..." he let his sentence trail off.

Waving a hand in front of her face as though swatting a fly, Lettie said, "Nonsense. I had a wonderful time today with both of you. I don't think I've ever had anyone clean my kitchen while I sat and enjoyed crocheting time." She picked up the loose cards, straightening them into a pile, and slid them into the box. "Just to let you know, I'm ready for an UNO rematch anytime you two are up for one."

"I believe we'll be taking you up on that offer real soon," Rob said. "How about we slide that small sofa in front of the fire and have a glass of wine. I brought a bottle in case you were interested. When Maggie falls asleep, she's out for hours."

"Sounds like a good plan," Lettie answered as her mouth went dry. *Is this really happening? After all these years, this guy shows up out of nowhere and is interested in me...who'd of thunk?*

"I'll move the sofa and stoke up the fire if you get the wine. I left it on the kitchen counter."

"Deal," she said.

She carried a bottle of wine, two wineglasses, and a couple of napkins as she tiptoed around the sleeping duo of dog and friend. By the time she got back, Rob had the love seat flanked with end tables.

"Some place to set our glasses," he nodded toward the tabletops as he reached out to help Lettie with the wine paraphernalia that she carried. Motioning toward the seat he said, "After you."

Small talk, small talk. Even though they sat in front of a lively fire, Lettie felt awkward and froze. *What to say, what to say?* She blurted out, "Great job on the fire. Do you have a fireplace?" *Oh my God, that was so lame!*

"Actually we do," Rob answered. "We have two in the house. One is a wood-burning stove as a backup for the furnace. We're out in the country too, so you know what that's like during a blizzard — the power can be out for hours, even days."

"Oh, yeah, there have been times where the only thing between us and freezing was that fireplace." Lettie pointed her chin to the brick structure.

Taking a sip, Rob asked, "Do you have any siblings or family around?"

Lettie raised her hand as though taking a pledge. "I'm guilty of being an only child. Parents are living the dream in Arizona. They come back at Christmas for a few weeks, and I usually go out there once or twice a year for a visit. There are a few cousins sprinkled around but no one I see on a regular basis. How about you?"

"It's just Mags and me. Dad passed away about eight years ago. He was a good guy. We both miss him a lot."

"And Mom?"

"I have no idea where she is." Rob studied the top of his wineglass for a beat. "She left when we were about ten months. She couldn't handle the, um...situation with my sister. So Dad raised us."

"I'm sorry," Lettie said.

"I figured out a long time ago that we were better off without her. Sometimes it sucked not having a mother, but

Dad loved us enough that we rarely noticed she didn't exist. I'm a lucky man for that."

"And your sister?"

"I'll never leave her," he said. "Not only did I promise Dad, but I just never could."

"You're so caring with her. I'm impressed."

"Maggie's one of the most loving and patient human beings you'll ever meet." He sipped his wine. "Besides, she really is an animal whisperer. She keeps the livestock in line."

"I can certainly vouch for her talent at communicating with Picasso, but livestock, seriously? What kind and how big?"

"Well, let's see...two horses of which you've met Dakota, then one goat, a coop full of chickens, one dog and two cats. One of the cats is a mouser for the barn and my body shop, while the other is a house cat that belongs to Maggie. The dog is a watch dog."

"My, that's quite a menagerie," Lettie said.

"Would you like to come by to meet the four-legged and feathery members of our family sometime?"

"I think I'd enjoy that," Lettie smiled. "I'd also love to see the setup you have for the body shop, and maybe teach Maggie a new stitch if she's ready."

"Well then, if I'm not being too forward, how does next weekend work for you?"

"It sounds perfect."

Rob stood to feed more logs onto the fire. Flames grew and sparks rose up the chimney.

"Now that I have you committed for the weekend, I suppose I should mention that I never got the Mustang on the bed of the tow truck today."

"It crossed my mind a few times," Lettie said.

"I guess I'll just have to come back for it another day. Maybe Wednesday?" he asked. "And this time I promise to not leave here without it."

Getting-to-know-each-other talk continued until shortly after ten o'clock when Rob suggested that he should get Maggie home and Lettie could be free of them. "I've really enjoyed myself tonight," he said. "I hope we haven't worn out our welcome."

"Absolutely not. You're both welcome anytime. I'd love to do it again." She paused for a moment and added, "Soon."

Rob put an arm around her shoulder and drew her toward him. With his other hand he traced her cheek and slowly they came together for a chaste kiss. Lettie ran her fingers to the back of his neck and their next kiss became longer and deeper.

When they finally broke apart, Lettie gulped air into her lungs. Her face felt flushed and not from the fire in the fireplace.

"Oh my," she said, then added, "That was fun."

Rob pushed his fingers through his hair and exhaled. "Whew, it sure was." He picked up her hand in both of his and said, "It might be best if we leave now, I wouldn't want to…" He squeezed her hand. "Don't misunderstand me, I've thoroughly enjoyed myself these last few nights. I could so easily, um…continue, but I'm not sure either of us is ready for it yet."

Lettie nodded. She agreed in theory, but the past few minutes of kissing him had literally taken her breath away. Squeezing his hand, she nodded again and said, "You're right."

The awkwardness dwindled as lights were turned on and they focused their attention to gathering the McKinnons' belongings. Rob made several trips to the truck and started the engine so it would be warm in the cab for Maggie.

Before he woke his sister, Rob took Lettie in his arms one last time. They held the embrace, enjoying the comfort of another human's touch, until Rob held her at arm's length. He gazed at her face and Lettie saw kindness and warmth in his eyes. "I've gotta go," he said. "But know that I don't want to."

"I don't want you to go either."

"I'm going to admit something that might sound silly. I was attracted to you the first time I saw you, when I lifted you into the sleigh. Do you remember that little excursion around the retreat before I brought you to the church?"

Lettie nodded.

"That was entirely a spur-of-the-moment impulse. I wanted to spend some time with you before I never saw you again." Rob bent and placed a kiss on her forehead. "Goodnight, Leticia. Sweet dreams."

Lettie was speechless and flushed with emotion. She watched as Rob awakened his sister, gently reminding her where they were and telling her they were heading home.

As her two guests walked past her at the doorway they each offered a brief thank-you hug. Rob added a peck on the cheek. All that remained of the evening were wonderful memories and the lingering scent of his cologne on her.

Chapter 19
Nedra

As always, Nedra was on time and prepared for the interview. Even though she knew quite well where the conference room was located, the receptionist walked her to the spot. When Joan swung open the door for her, she whispered, "Good luck, Nedra. We all hope you're going to get the position." In a louder voice she said, "Please take a seat, Ms. Lange. The committee will be with you in a minute."

"Thank you, Joan."

Sitting at what she deemed an appropriate place at the long table, Nedra calmed her nerves by retrieving papers from her briefcase and organizing them in front of her. Moments later, the door opened and a woman and two men came through the door. They each shook hands with her before sitting down.

The female conducted the interview, with the men interjecting questions occasionally. Nedra slid a copy of her resume to each person at the correct time and thought the interview was going quite well. About eight minutes had passed when Ms. Schmidt said, "Well, I think we have everything we need to make a decision."

Nedra hid her shock. An interview of this type should last longer than eight minutes and there should be much more information shared between the two parties. Nothing was said about responsibilities or expectations. Not a word was whispered about benefits or salary. Not a hint of the universally common question: Where do you see yourself in five years?

Could they be assuming that I already know what the responsibilities entail? It seemed very unprofessional on their part. *Maybe they're simply new at this.*

"I have a few questions," Nedra said. She started with a basic one, "When would I be expected to start?" She wanted to make it clear that she was prepared to terminate her six-month leave of absence if necessary.

After that was satisfactorily answered, she asked another question, "If I'm offered the position, will my assistant, Kathy, be moved to take over my current job?"

This question-and-answer period went on for a few minutes, but with only half of her queries asked, Ms. Schmidt rose and stated, "It was a pleasure meeting you, Nedra. We've heard many wonderful things about you. We will make our decision today and notify you via phone or email. I'm sorry if I seem abrupt, but we have a plane to catch back to New York. We all thank you for your time."

Nedra felt relief as she smiled and once again shook the hands of these three people. *So that was why the interview seemed rushed…they had a plane to catch.*

On her way out of the conference room she stopped by her office to see Kathy.

"How'd it go?" Kathy was eager to hear what happened.

"Well, I think it went okay. It was shorter than I would have expected, but I guess they're aware of my work and abilities since I've been here so long."

Kathy spoke with a hushed voice. "Including you, they interviewed a total of four people. They were very fast with all of them, so don't worry. None of them were more than ten minutes in and out." Kathy sliced her hand through the air. "I still think you've got this."

"They said HR would contact me this afternoon. They want a quick and smooth transition," Nedra told her fellow worker. "I let them know that I could definitely give them what they were looking for."

"Are you staying today?" Kathy asked.

"No. I don't want it to look like I'm hanging around for

any reason. I think it would be unprofessional."

"I guess you're right. Keep me posted when you hear something," Kathy said, and gave Nedra a hug. "Boy, I miss you around here."

"It's funny, but I kind of miss it around here, too."

By the time her train pulled away from Millennium Station, Nedra was feeling positive again. She checked her emails, but there was nothing from HR. She did however have a text message from Lettie:

OMG can't believe what's happening to the MQR. Checked the blog etc YES I'LL BE AT THE MEETING! Sorry but didn't have phone with me yesterday. Just saw this right now.

Nedra answered:

Leaving Chi now. Be home soon. Glad you'll be there tomorrow. We need to show support. Our social media is blowing up. Lots of support from quilters around the country. Phree's a wreck.

Marge joined in on the group message:

The guests took a vote. We're loading up busses tomorrow and bringing ALL to the meeting! Can't wait to see look on committee's faces =)

Helen joined in:

Nedra, I covered for you like we discussed on social media while you were in city. People are emailing & contacting those bastards like crazy. We are officially the squeaky wheel in Whitney! How'd the interview go?

Texts flew back and forth until Nedra texted a white lie:

Pulling in to Whitney. Gotta go.

Nedra hoped to check her emails again, and have a few quiet moments to think about the interview before she reached home. Home. She wasn't sure she wanted to be there alone, anxiously pacing around the whole house while she waited for a call that would determine her future. Nate was working on a project so he wasn't available, the same with Brian. She *really* didn't need any more fabric for any reason, therapeutic or not, so there was no point in heading to the Quilter's Closet.

I'll head over to the retreat and tend to the social media sites. It will feel good to be among friends.

Chapter 20
Brian

Eminent domain was not Brian's specialty. He was a general law guy and knew a little bit about a lot of things and a whole lot about a few things. Eminent domain landed in the first category. He did, however, have the combined knowledge of his partners and a friend in the city whose specialty was none other.

Lisa returned his call right away. "What's up, big guy?"

"I need to pick your brain," he said, and explained the situation happening at the MQR.

"Once that Notice of Intent to Appraise letter hit the streets on Saturday, I've become a very popular person around here. The Interstate 80 bypass is going to cut a long swath through the south end of the county and well into Indiana, a lot of it being farmland. What's your client got?"

Brian explained the situation at the Mayflower Quilters Retreat.

"From what I can gather about the situation, there are two different routes proposed," Lisa said. "But at this point only one has been made public. They're only a mile apart, which doesn't sound like much but rumor has it that Proposal One is more invasive to the landowners, and Proposal Two is less invasive to the landowners but adds more costs and time to the construction, specifically in the number of bridges needed."

"That adds a little hope for my client," Brian said. "It's also my understanding that there's no way to negotiate in an eminent domain situation and absolutely no way out of the land grab." Brian was looking for clarification. "Is that correct?"

"That about sums it up, counselor. The only thing negotiable is how much money will change hands."

"That's what I was afraid of. Any suggestions when we go before the meeting tomorrow?"

"Yeah, push for Proposal Two if that helps your client," Lisa said. "I'll email you a link that clarifies the properties involved in Prop Two, and further describes which parcels will be affected. Also, try to get together a strong coalition to sway them to go the other way."

Brian sighed, "Unfortunately, there's not a lot of time for that."

"And that is exactly why they move so fast."

"Thanks for your help, Lisa...you're the best."

"Anytime, Mr. Barber. Keep me posted."

Seconds after Brian hung up, his assistant buzzed him. "There's a Rosa Mitchell on line four."

"I've got it." Pushing the flashing red button on his phone panel, Brian said, "Hi Rosa. What can I do for you?"

"I've got three names," she said. "I know who stole Lettie's car and beat Picasso, but I won't give them to you unless you can promise me that you won't involve Ricky."

"I take it Ricky shared the information with you." Brian pulled a tablet of paper in front of him. "How did he find out?"

"He overheard one of the guys bragging to a group of kids in the locker room."

"Was this guy aware that Ricky heard him?"

"He doesn't think so."

"I'm guessing that simply by telling even only one person, he started a ripple effect. By now most of the school knows who the guilty party is. I'd guess that Ricky will be free from suspicion. That's the beauty of kids doing something illegal...they can't help but brag about their accomplishments. Give me the names and I'll contact the police. They'll no doubt pit the three of them against each other and those creeps will rat each other out for the possibility of a lighter sentence."

"What do you think Lettie will do?"

"That's what I'm most worried about."

Chapter 21
Lettie

After hearing the news about the possible eminent domain takeover of the MQR, Lettie was enraged. *First my car, then my dog, now the quilt retreat...what's next?* And January wasn't even over yet!

Feeling distracted (in a good way) from time spent with Rob this past weekend, Lettie thought it might be worthwhile to head to the retreat and, face to face with Marge and whoever else might be there, hear the most current information on the 'land grab'. What would this mean for the retreat? Was there any recourse or would their beloved Mayflower Quilters Retreat be bulldozed only to be replaced with a freeway?

Putting on her coat and miscellaneous outerwear, Lettie thought it might be a good idea to let Picasso go outside for a potty break before she left home. This would be the first time her sweet baby would be alone since the attack, and Lettie didn't intend to be gone very long. Large thick snowflakes were falling and she didn't want him wandering around outside when she wasn't there. Lettie made sure the doggy door was blocked and he was unable to get out on his own.

When she had spent a sufficient amount of time saying goodbye to him, Lettie screwed up her courage and with one final kiss, set the security system and walked out the front door. This whole process of allowing him to be alone was way harder to do than she had thought it would be. *Next time it simply has to be easier.*

When she arrived at the MQR, she pulled into the employee parking lot at the back end of the building. Lettie noticed Nedra's car was there and another vehicle that she believed belonged to Brian. The maintenance crew was hand shoveling the sidewalks and spreading salt on the cleared paths, but the snow was coming down so fast the walkways were immediately covered over again. Lettie held her coat collar tight around her neck and waving to Steve Bonini, she called out, "Looks like you've got your hands full for a while."

"They're saying three to five inches, so it shouldn't be too big of a deal," he called back.

Laughing Lettie said, "Hang in there. Spring is only a few months away."

Steve gave her the thumbs up sign and lowered his head to his work.

The crew would soon need to get the Gators out and plow the sidewalks instead of doing it by hand. She could hear the pickups already plowing the parking areas and the long driveway. This wonderful place truly was a haven for so many reasons. It employed numerous people who were both happy and grateful for their jobs. What a shameful thing it would be to see the retreat destroyed. Surely there must be another way.

Lettie heard laughter and squeals. As she walked around the corner of the retreat, three women were having a snowball fight and three others were attempting to make a snowman with the little bit of snow that had fallen. Approaching the snowy merrymakers, she could see that their cheeks were pink with cold and exhilaration, and they all shared the same mischievous smiles.

In a long southern drawl one of the snowball throwers called out to her, "We're from Southern Mississippi, down by the Gulf, and we've never played in snow before!" She threw a badly made snowball that fell apart before it even came close to its target. "This is so much fun!"

Lettie left the cleared sidewalk and moved toward the women. "Let me give you a few pointers." Walking them through the fine art of snowball making, she said, "Scoop two big handfuls from the ground or car or wherever." She showed them. "Now this is the important part…you've got to pack it tight." All six heads bent over her hands as though she were giving a lesson in free motion quilting to a group of beginners. "Find the perfect target and let it rip." Lettie threw hard and true as her flying white orb hit a tree trunk dead center.

The women cheered her remarkable ability with *oohs* and *ahs*.

"I knew we were doing something wrong, but couldn't figure out why it kept falling apart," said one of the women.

"Glad I could be of assistance," Lettie laughed. "We're supposed to get up to five inches of this stuff so you might want to pace yourselves." While they were sufficiently bundled up, these Southern Belles weren't used to the cold and Lettie didn't want them to experience their first bout of frostbite.

The sidetracked quilters each bent over for fistfuls of snow. As Lettie headed back to the sidewalk she could hear the muffled sound of gloved hands packing snowballs. She called out, "Have fun, ladies, but take care not to get too cold."

Outside the door to the MQR, Lettie stomped her feet on the oversized welcome mat. Marge was alone in her office, which was fondly called the Bridge. The nickname helped to keep the illusion alive of being on a ship. She looked up when Lettie entered.

"I saw you giving a tutorial on snowball making," Marge said. "Those six women were so darn worked up when the first flakes came down. You'd have thought it was snowing fabric."

Lettie laughed. "I kind of felt sorry for them when I saw they were throwing handfuls of snow at each other. I figured it was time to give them a lesson."

Looking out the window of the Bridge and badly mimicking a southern accent, Marge said, "I think y'all did a mighty fine job, by golly." Back to her Chicago accent, she added, "What brings you here today, my dear?"

"I'm hoping to learn about this eminent domain thing that's going on," she answered and sat in a chair across from Marge's desk, shrugging her arms out of her coat. "I was out of the loop yesterday when all the info was being texted, so I didn't learn about it until I looked at my phone this morning."

"The first thing you need to know is that Phree is near hysteria." Marge shook her head. "I'm talking DEFCON 1. Poor girl, I really feel sorry for her. She finally achieves her dream of owning this place, and it looks like it might get yanked out from under her." She paused and asked, "What were you doing that you missed all those texts?"

"Nothing special. My phone died and I didn't notice it until today." Lettie knew it was a lame excuse but couldn't think fast enough for a believable answer. She wasn't ready to share her weekend rendezvous with Rob just yet.

Marge gave her the stink eye. It was clear she wasn't buying the excuse.

"Brian, Phree, and Sunnie are in the conference room right now going over the details," Marge said. "So we'll have to wait until they're finished to learn what the plan is…if there is a plan."

"I saw Nedra's car out there. Where's she at?"

"Nedra is also near hysteria but for different reasons. Right now she's in the Brewster Room attempting to get her mind off this morning's interview at *Excel*. Poor girl is convinced it didn't go well, but I think she's just buying trouble. I'd be stunned if she didn't get the position. HR is going to call or email her this afternoon and she doesn't want to be home alone when they contact her."

"I can understand that," Lettie said. "Tell me about this meeting tomorrow night for the eminent domain thingy."

"We're trying to get a groundswell of support *for* the retreat and *against* the proposal. I'm not mentioning this part to Phree, but it sounds like it won't do any good. However, if we make a big enough stink," Marge spread her hands in front of her and shrugged her shoulders, "who knows what might happen?"

Phree, eyes red and swollen, entered the office. Sunnie had her arm around her distressed daughter's waist. Brian was right behind them.

"What's the verdict?" Marge asked.

"I'm sorry, Marge, but I can't hear this again." Phree was barely holding it together. "I'm heading home to take a nap. Brian can tell you."

In a completely hushed room, Phree gathered up her outerwear from the closet.

As she passed Brian he gave her shoulder a squeeze. "Hang in there, Phree. Remember there's always hope this will work out."

Lettie embraced her without a word. As they broke apart she said, "I'm praying for you." This made Phree choke back a sob. Clearly too upset to talk, she simply nodded her thanks.

"Come on, honey," Sunnie said, "let's get you home. A hot cup of tea and a nap will make you feel better. I'll stay with you as long as you need me."

"Use the side door," Marge said. "We have some high-spirited first-time Southerners playing in the snow out front."

Marge, as always, was on top of every situation.

When mother and daughter were out of earshot, Lettie asked softly, "Is there really any hope for the retreat?"

Brian rubbed a hand over his chin and eventually answered. "We're sure going to try."

"What gives?" Marge asked.

Brian described how he was going to push as hard as possible for the committee to move forward with the other proposal. Prop 2, as it was being called, would include the southernmost tip of Phree's property—a section of wooded land that was well away from the retreat. He explained that cost was the reason the government favored Prop 1. "They'll have to foot the bill for at least five more bridges if they go the other route," he said. "Either way Phree will lose land, but Prop 2 is more retreat friendly. It's far enough away not to be seen and noise won't be a factor at that distance either."

"So what needs to be done?" Marge asked.

"I'll prepare an argument and present it at the meeting. If a few people show up to protest, that might help. If a lot of people show up to protest…it might help a lot more."

"Every quilter here this week is horrified with the proposal. We'll be bringing several shuttles full of supporters, including a ninety-eight-year-old lifetime quilter," Marge said. "All the employees that are not absolutely needed here tonight will be joining us, too. We've also received many emails, tweets, and Facebook posts from fans of the retreat stating that they contacted the committee with their concerns."

"That's excellent work. I can't say it will help, but I know it can't hurt to show massive support for the MQR." Brian made a note on his tablet. "I'll have my secretary contact some of the television stations. Your ninety-eight-year-old quilter might turn out to be quite a draw."

Marge said, "You've given me hope."

And Lettie had to agree.

"If you'll excuse me, ladies, I need to get to the office and work on my argument." Brian hoisted his frame from the chair. "But if you've got a minute, Lettie, I'd like to speak to you in private. Is it okay if we use the conference room, Marge?"

Lettie had no idea where this was going, but answered, "Sure. Let's do it."

They were silent on the walk to the conference room. Lettie was both curious and concerned. *What could this be about? Maybe my car?*

Brian closed the door behind them and said, "Have a seat." After she chose a chair, he sat next to her and pivoted his chair to face her.

"You're starting to scare me," she said with a nervous laugh.

He picked up one of her hands and held it in both of his. "I was given three names."

Lettie felt her face drain but said nothing.

"I passed them on to the police. They'll pick up the juveniles and take them in for questioning after school today."

Lettie's whole body trembled. "Who?"

"I think it's best not to tell you at this moment in case this proves to be an incorrect accusation. But the minute they're arrested, I'll let you know. I can tell you that they're Whitney High School students."

Anger and relief mingled, but anger won the battle. "They need to be held accountable for what they did to Picasso." With no tissue in sight, she wiped at a tear with her sleeve. "I want to press charges. I'll *never* forgive them. Never."

"That's exactly what I thought you'd say. But, let's wait to see what the police find out. For now, go home and be happy Picasso is still alive and improving. If these are the culprits, we'll know soon enough."

On the way back to the Bridge, Nedra was walking toward them. Lettie took one look at her face and knew her friend had received bad news.

Chapter 22
Nedra

A trip to the Brewster Quilters Room was exactly the medicine that Nedra needed. The mood among the quilters was joyful and upbeat. Pure bliss surrounded her and made it difficult to continue her sense of gloom and defeat. She sat for a while with the hand stitchers sipping tea and listening to a woman from Kansas who was taking a break from quilting in order to finish a long overdue knitting project. Donna was sharing an animated tale about when her husband discovered her hidden stash of fabric.

From there, Nedra wandered between the stations of quilters whose projects were all at various stages of completion. Eager to introduce herself to Irma, the eldest quilter to ever be a guest at the MQR, she was disappointed to learn the nonagenarian was taking a nap. Nedra had just finished chatting with someone who was working on a baby quilt for their twelfth grandchild, when she spotted a woman machine-piecing an elaborate quilt done with Civil War reproduction fabrics. Before she could get to the quilter, her cell phone vibrated. A peek at the screen told her it was coming from the offices at *Excel*.

Making a beeline for the quiet hall just outside the door of the Brewster Room, Nedra tapped the answer button and said, "Hello." Blessedly the hallway was empty as well as all of the benches and chairs. She chose a comfortable occasional chair and sat down.

"May I speak with Nedra Lange, please?"

"This is Nedra."

"Nedra, this is Samantha from Human Resources at *Excel Chicago*, I'm calling in regard to the position for which   you   interviewed   earlier   today."

"Yes..."

"I'm sorry to have to inform you, Nedra, that you were not chosen for the position."

Nedra felt her stomach clench. The small amount of food which it held rose and left the taste of bile in her mouth. She said nothing.

"Again, I'm sorry, Nedra," Samantha's voice turned fake apologetic, "but the company is willing to offer you a handsome severance package since your services will no longer be required."

"What? What do you mean severance package?" Nedra heard her voice rise in disbelief. "Am I being let go?"

"Yes. I'm so very sorry. The new editor-in-chief will be bringing his own support staff with him."

"There must be some mistake." Nedra squeezed her eyes closed as her incredulity turned to anger. "I've been at that magazine for almost twenty years, and most of them as assistant editor...and you're telling me I'm being fired?"

"We prefer to think of it as being replaced."

"What about Kathy my assistant? Is she also *being replaced*?"

"I'm not at liberty to discuss the status of another employee with you, Ms. Lange."

Nedra wanted to scream, but instead tears of frustration rolled down her cheeks.

"As I said..." Samantha sighed and sounded impatient. "Corporate has been very generous and you'll be receiving quite a nice severance package. I can go over it with you if you wish, but everything is spelled out in the email I'm sending you."

At this point, Nedra was boiling hot and began to pace as her fury built. "All I can say is this offer better be very generous. Email me the proposal and I'll run it past my lawyer."

"It's on its way right now. Again I'm sorr..."

Nedra cut her off. "Samantha, you can call it being replaced if that makes you feel better about yourself, but I suggest it's more like being screwed! If Don were alive, he'd be mortified by what's going on there."

"Everything you need to know about vacating your office will be in the email. If you don't have any more questions, I'll..."

Nedra disconnected the call before simpering Samantha could once again tell Nedra how sorry she was. Prim, proper, and exquisitely dressed Nedra Lange looked at the blank screen of her cell phone and quietly said, "Kiss my ass."

The atmosphere of peace and happiness she had felt with a roomful of quilters only moments earlier had dissolved into sorrow. Walking toward the Bridge, Nedra saw Lettie and Brian leaving the conference room. All three stopped and stared down the hall at each other. Nedra knew the moment her quilting sister saw her distress as she moved toward her. No words were shared but rather an embrace said it all. Grateful and in need of a hug, she allowed some of Lettie's strength to fortify her against the sadness that she now felt deep in her bones.

"I'm sorry," Lettie said. "Will you stay on as assistant?"

"They fired me."

"What?"

"They let me go with a severance package." Nedra dabbed at her eyes. "I don't know what I'm going to do."

Brian stayed back as the friends conversed, but he heard everything his sister said. "Nedra, I'm so sorry," he said as he pulled her toward him and bent to kiss her forehead. "Is there anything I can do to help?"

"Right now I'm completely numb," she said. "But I sure could go for a stiff drink or two...maybe followed by some wine."

"You got it, sis," Brian said. "You name the time and place."

"Now and my house."

Brian asked, "Are you in, Lettie?"

"I'd love to but I need to get home for Picasso. He has several medications that I need to get in him at different hours during the evening." Lettie rubbed her friend's arm, as if to take off the chill.

"I'll be okay with my little brother until Nate can get there. You can be sure they'll both help to get my head on straight." Nedra smiled.

"If you need anything, Ned, just call me...I'll make it work and be there."

"Thanks, I know you will."

They walked toward the Bridge to share the bad news with Marge, and then each would go their separate ways.

Chapter 23
Lettie

Picasso greeted Lettie with a whimper. He had to go out. With about four inches of fresh snow on the ground, it appeared that the storm would last another few hours. By that time the total accumulation was upgraded to around seven inches. Without taking her coat off, Lettie opened the door for Picasso. "Come on, boy. Let's do this fast. It's nasty out there."

Taking hold of the snow shovel that she kept near the front door, Lettie cleared a narrow path for her dog and continued to shovel a small area where he could do his business. The chore was finished in a matter of minutes and both of them hurried inside to dry out and warm up. Lettie had just finished toweling off Picasso and checking that his cast was dry when her cell chirped a notification that she had received a text.

> *Mags and I are leaving in five minutes to plow your driveway and parking area. If you're not home, no problem. If you are, want to share some Chinese with us?*

Lettie didn't need to think twice and keyed in:

> *YES!! I love Chinese!*

He answered:

> *Great! Any preferences?*

A most unusual feeling came over her…one of being appreciated and valued. A broad grin brightened Lettie's face as she tapped the keys on her phone.

> *Anything is fine. Surprise me!*

She told Picasso, "We're going to have company again tonight, old boy. Waddya think of that?"

It didn't take long before old demons crept their way into Lettie's mind. *What the heck do I think is going to happen with this guy? It's going to end like all the rest...I'll push him away.* But she continued to tidy up the living room, light a few candles, build the perfect log pyramid in the fireplace, fluff up the pillows, and try on three sweaters before deciding which looked best.

Even though I have no interest in a relationship with Rob, it can't hurt to have my home look inviting and me looking...well, hot.

By the time she reached the kitchen where she set a stack of dinner plates and utensils on the table, she was determined to distance herself from any possibility of leading him on. The faint scraping of a snowplow invaded the quiet and drew near. He was here. Lettie pumped her fist and said, "Yes!"

Possibly for the first time since that horrendous experience with her fiancé, Lettie realized that her past might have no power over her feelings for Robert McKinnon.

The pickup was driven as close to the house as possible. The passenger door opened and Maggie's short legs skillfully took her from the running board of the truck to the snow covered ground. Carefully choosing her steps on the snowy gravel, arms slightly outstretched for balance, she plodded toward the farmhouse. When she spotted Lettie holding the door open, she halted her progress and waved with her whole arm. "Lettie," she called out smiling. "Hi. I'm coming."

"Take your time, Maggie." Lettie's heart melted as she watched her new friend having to work so hard for what came so easy to others. "Be careful, it's slippery out there."

Stopping again, Maggie said, "How does Picasso feel?"

"He feels great and he can't wait to see you," Lettie answered.

It was at this time that Picasso decided to see what was taking place and who was at his front door. Appearing at Lettie's side, the old boy must have approved because his tail beat against her legs as he whined. Eventually he let loose with a friendly bark just as Maggie made it onto the porch. Holding onto his collar, Lettie held him back. In his exuberance she was fearful that he could easily knock Maggie to the ground on the slippery wooden porch.

"Hang on, buddy, she'll be here soon." This was the most excited and the most 'normal' she had seen him since he came home from the vet's. With more than a little manipulation of the dog, the door, and Maggie, Lettie was able to get them all safely inside.

Immediately falling to her knees, Maggie wrapped her arms around the excited shepherd. There were sloppy dog kisses and giggles—not to mention a feel-good smile on Lettie's face. She eventually said, "All right, you two. We need to get Miss Maggie's wet coat off so she can warm up a little."

With red cheeks, rosy from the cold, Maggie said, "Oh. Rob is plowing your parking lot. He'll be in when he's done."

"Okay," Lettie responded. "It was really nice of both of you to come out in the storm and plow my snow."

"It was my idea," Maggie said with pride. "Robbie thought of the food." Her boots and coat came off with some doing...but Maggie got the job done by herself.

"You two are quite the team."

"Yes, we are. Did you know we're twins?"

"I did. I bet it's cool to have a twin." Lettie slipped her arm around Maggie's shoulders. "Let's go by the fire and warm you up."

When Rob came in with a large brown paper bag of food, his sister was snuggling with Picasso, petting him while Lettie was coming from the kitchen carrying two mugs and a carafe.

"Welcome, and thank you," she said to Rob and held up a mug. "Would you like some hot chocolate? I made a full carafe."

"Sounds perfect," he answered. "I hope we aren't intruding in any way."

"Not at all."

As Rob retrieved one aromatic container bulging with food after another from the paper bag, Lettie said, "How many people are we expecting tonight?"

He laughed. "Chinese makes for great leftovers."

Snow continued to fall as the activities of the evening were repeated the same as they were on Sunday night— dinner, a round of UNO, Maddie cuddling with Picasso on the sofa and eventually falling asleep, and Lettie and Rob in front of the fire. The only difference was that it didn't take him all night to put his arm around her.

"Thank you for accepting Maggie," he said.

"Why wouldn't I? She's fantastic."

Rob picked at a thread on his sweater. "Not everyone feels that way."

"Well," Lettie said. "Then it sucks to be them."

Rob shook his head. "I'll never leave her for any reason."

Feeling this might be a warning, Lettie nonetheless said, "As it should be. Tell me about the McKinnon twins."

He leaned away from her and held her gaze. "Are you sure?"

"Very much sure."

"Then I'll keep it short, but tell you everything."

Neither Rob nor Maggie had any memories of their mother. Long before the days of ultrasound and amniocentesis, Alice McKinnon had no idea she was pregnant with twins and that one of them would be born with Down syndrome. He knew from stories that she was twenty-three years old when she delivered her babies. He had, at a much older age, been informed that their mother walked out on her new family when the babies were ten months old. Apparently, Alice simply could not handle the fact that her baby girl was a child with Down syndrome.

When Rob's crying had turned to screaming that night, his father rose to see if Alice needed help feeding the babies. At some point during the night, she had left a note propped on the changing table in the nursery. It simply stated: 'I can't do this. I don't know how to love Margaret. I pray you all forgive me.'

"So Dad took it from there," he said. "I've always suspected that in the beginning he hoped she'd come back. But at some point for him, the three of us became the norm. Since Maggie and I never knew the difference, not having Alice around *was* the norm...but that doesn't mean we didn't miss having a mother." Rob locked his fingers behind his head, elbows pointing like wings. After purging his thoughts with a deep puff of breath he said, "Getting back on track with the short version of this story, I gotta say that I admired my dad so much. He was a hell of a role model for me."

Lettie learned that Robert Senior instilled in Maggie that she was perfect just the way she was, that he loved her to the ends of the earth, and that she was Daddy's favorite girl.

"And you? What did he tell you?" Lettie asked.

"Similar things except for the 'favorite girl' part." They both laughed and then Rob smiled and wistfully said, "I was his best buddy."

"He sounds like a good man. I wish I could have known him." Lettie truly wanted to believe that there was a good man for her somewhere in the world. *Could he perhaps be sitting in my living room right now?*

"I know I run the risk of sounding as though I'm somewhere between being defensive or a bragger, but my sister is really a wonderful, kind person, and very smart to boot."

Lettie threw up her hands and shook her head. "You don't have to convince me," she said. "I've seen it with my own eyes."

"That's kind of you."

"It's true," Lettie said. "She picked up that crochet stitch instantly and the way she communicates with Picasso is enviable."

He drew her closer and kissed the top of her head. Several minutes passed and Lettie enjoyed the closeness of being held, the warmth, and the manly smell of his cologne.

"My father told me that I should always look out for my sister. He said that if the tables were turned, he'd expect the same of her."

"Some might say he gave you a heavy burden," Lettie said. "It might even cause resentment."

"Not for me. You see, she's my twin. We have that bond between us. I can't explain it but it's impossible to ignore. I've found out the hard way that others can feel bitter about what Mags and I share."

Lettie thought she knew where this was going, so she said, "Do you feel you've had to forfeit things to live up to your promise? Were you ever married...or in a relationship?" She wondered if she had been too brazen but also sought to find out if there was an additional obligation to being involved with him.

"A couple of years before Dad passed away...let's see, I guess it's been about ten years ago, I was engaged. I was thirty-seven. Unfortunately, I had never discussed my commitment to my sister with my fiancé. Cindy was always appropriately polite with Maggie, but their relationship was cool and somewhat distant. Looking back I'd say that was putting it mildly," Rob smirked. "Anyway, we were about three months from the wedding date and the subject came up when we were house hunting. I told her we'd have to calculate space for Maggie for after Dad died." Shaking his head at the memory, Rob continued. "She simply said, 'That's not going to happen.' Honestly, Lettie, I was dumbstruck. I asked her, 'What do you think is going to happen with

Maggie at that point?' And do you know what she said?"

"I'm fearful that I might have an idea what it was."

"She told me that we would find a nice home for retarded people where she could live with others just like her and be happy. She actually used the word 'retarded'. I *hate* that word. That word does *not* sum up my sister or 'others like her.' I told Cindy right there that I didn't think I could marry her. She cried and apologized and vowed that Maggie could live with us but I couldn't take the chance that she would betray her promise to me. I had a strong premonition that I would have to cut ties with her either before the wedding or soon after Dad died...you know, pay now or pay later. So why even go there?"

Rob looked over his shoulder at his sleeping sister. "At this point it's just the two of us. I can't leave her alone, Lettie. I won't."

"I'm sorry that it didn't work out for you," Lettie said, and then she added, "well, not really. If it had worked out the two of you wouldn't be here, and I'm really happy that you are."

He pulled her in for a chaste kiss and then said, "What about you? Have you ever been engaged or married? Any children?"

She laughed and said, "Yes, no, and no."

Lettie had never shared a portion of her past with even her closest friends. It wasn't that she feared her Bunco and quilting friends would think less of her, rather she couldn't face the humiliation again. Yet, here she was ready to blab to Rob about the most embarrassing part of her life. Confessing her most shameful story to a guy she met when he drove her around in a sleigh and then came to tow her damaged car...did that seem anywhere near sensible? *But then again, people meet in all kinds of weird ways, so really, what difference does it make how we met?* The only thing that mattered was: Could she trust him not to hurt her?

She hesitated to continue her verbal memoir. If Rob didn't push her to keep going, she would drop it. There was a long silence as she studied the flames in the fireplace, determining whether or not this guy, whose arm was around her, could go the distance and change her bitterness.

Finally Rob said, "Well?"

So she started. She told him about Eric. She told him everything about their messed up relationship. She told him of her wedding day and how he never showed up for the ceremony, explaining in detail just how much being jilted at the church had hurt and humiliated her. She told him how it had poisoned her ability to trust a man and ruined any relationship that she ever dared to start.

"I wonder what our lives would have been like if we had married back then," she said. "I'm pretty sure I would have been miserable."

"And I'm pretty sure that ultimately I would have made Cindy miserable because of my commitment to Maggie." He kissed her hair. "For what it's worth, Eric sounds like an 'A Number One Jerk.' And while it's easy for me to say, I'm glad he was stupid enough not to show up that day. I think he did you a favor."

"I was just thinking the same about you. It seems that you dodged a mighty big bullet, mister."

After Rob walked a sleepy Maggie to the truck, he came back to the house to say a final goodnight to Lettie. "Is it still okay if we get the Mustang on Wednesday? I'd do it tomorrow but I have a meeting that I have to attend after work."

"That'll be fine. I'm busy with retreat stuff tomorrow night anyway."

"I promise to get your Mustang on the bed of the wrecker this time." Rob laughed and shyly confessed, "I will admit that by not picking up your car, I had a good reason to come back a few more times."

Lettie thought that might have been the most romantic thing said to her in a long time. Feeling herself blush, she said, "I'm flattered."

The horn of the truck sounded a short honk and they both laughed. "I guess someone's getting impatient to get home," Rob said.

"Until Wednesday then," Lettie said softly.

"One more thing." Rob pulled her into his embrace. "I think it's good that we each know what we're up against." He took her by the shoulders and looking her square in the eyes said, "I want you to be prepared that I'm personally going to take the time to prove to you that all men aren't losers."

Chapter 24
Nedra

The visit from her brother and then Nate, a few drinks, a little wine, some carryout food, and what felt like a never-ending crying jag summed up Nedra's day yesterday. Nate spent the night listening to her fears and bitter resentment over being fired while consoling her with reassurance that the situation would work itself out. He now busied himself in the kitchen making coffee and toast before leaving for work.

Approaching him from behind as he slathered a thin smear of butter over the toast, Nedra leaned into him and wrapped her arms around his waist while resting her cheek on his back. "Thank you for everything," she said. "I apologize for being a pain in the butt."

Nate turned and embraced her. "Under the circumstances, I'd say you handled everything quite well."

"Liar," she said. "I did not."

"Don't be too hard on yourself, Ned. Most people would have reacted the same way. To unexpectedly lose a job is traumatizing at best, especially when you have worked there for as long as you have."

"Well, I'm not a big fan of wallowing," she told him. "I'd rather take charge and move forward. So, I'm declaring that my pity party is officially over. Worse things can happen in life, right?"

"That's true, but don't minimize what they did to you. This was a bad one," Nate said.

"I'm going to be fine, really I am. When you leave I'm going to take a nice long shower, get dressed, and get going on that novel. I've got some new ideas that I want to work on."

"Great," he said with much enthusiasm. "I look forward to reading it when you're ready to share."

"As much as I'd love for you to stay all day, it's time for you to get to work," she said. "Your first appointment will be kept waiting if you don't get going."

"If you're sure you're okay?" he questioned with eyebrows raised.

"Absolutely. The sooner you leave the sooner I can get to work on my laptop."

"I'll be by about six tonight to pick you up for the meeting."

They strolled to the door arm in arm where Nate shrugged into his coat and gloves. "Go get that toast in you. You'll feel better with some food in your tummy." He bent to kiss her. "Goodbye." Another peck, and he added, "I love you."

"Love you, too," she replied.

After he exited she locked the door, pulled her robe sash tight around her waist, and headed for the kitchen. Once there, she retrieved a bottle of wine from the wine refrigerator, snagged a clean wineglass from the cabinet, and with her slippers making a scuffing sound she wandered toward the stairs and her bedroom. She had a plan all right, but it had nothing to do with writing.

Only a smidgen of guilt for deceiving Nate worked its way into Nedra's bruised psyche. She rationalized her lies by telling herself that she had saved him a day of worry. What was even worse was the fear that he might have chosen to cancel his appointments and spend the day fussing over her. She'd pull it together at some point, but today she wanted to be left alone. There was still a good amount of crying that needed to be done, and she hadn't finished worrying about how she would spend her days now that she was unemployed.

After unplugging her landline, Nedra powered off her

cell phone. The pity party wasn't over yet.

The persistent sound of a doorbell finally broke through Nedra's stupor. Who in the world could it be at this time of night? Then her Mommy Radar kicked in...oh my God, the girls. Never had a person disengaged from a jumble of bedclothes and a tangled bathrobe quicker. Racing down the stairs barefooted, she threw the door open without looking through the peephole. Nate stood before her, finger pushing the button to a fresh wave of chiming.

"What's going on? What time is it?" she asked.

Nate answered, "Time we were on our way to the eminent domain meeting."

"Oh, no. I must have fallen asleep," she said. "Give me a minute, I'll be right down." And up the stairs she flew.

A two-minute shower was in order, along with some major tooth brushing. She'd go without makeup but wouldn't skip her face cream. Slacks, sweater, shoes, fluff hair, spritz perfume—she was ready.

Downstairs she found Nate in the kitchen staring at the toast and coffee he had made for her ten hours ago.

"I'm ready," she said in a singsong voice. "I guess we need to get going."

"I guess we do," he answered, holding the door open for her.

Nedra could tell by his voice and mannerisms that he was angry and most likely felt betrayed as well. After he pulled the car out of the driveway, it was time for another lie. As cheerfully as she could manage she said, "I'm really sorry about that, Nate. I worked all day on the manuscript and somewhere around...oh, I don't know, about three o'clock I took a nap. I intended for it to be a catnap, but I guess I was more tired than I realized. I probably should have set an alarm."

"Is this how it's going to be?" Nate asked.

Acting confused she said, "What do you mean?"

"That we're going to start lying to each other."

Nedra began to stutter an excuse, then slumped against the door and gazed out the car's window. When it was clear that Nate was waiting for her to talk, she said in a small voice, "I'm ashamed in so many ways. I feel as though twenty years of my life have been discredited and it's been nothing more than a joke." Now that she started expressing her feelings, she couldn't stop. "I'm not going to lie, it would have hurt not being offered Don's position, but to be let go, fired, replaced, call it what you want, it fills me with shame. I was darn good at what I did, Nate...darn good. Not only was I good at my job, but I loved working. That's the hardest part. I loved everything about it. And now it's gone."

Somewhere in the middle of her rant, tears began to fall. "I have absolutely no idea what I'm going to do. I mean none whatsoever. Can you recognize how devastating that is?" Swiping at her eyes, she continued, "Don't even go there about that stupid novel I'm pretending to write. I don't like the story I came up with. I also don't like the fact that I have to come up with hundreds of pages that somehow all tie together and tell a compelling story. Do you have any idea how hard that is? It terrifies me. I'm used to writing article length stories for a magazine. A new assignment every week means a fresh challenge and fresh ideas."

Nate drove his car into the high school parking lot; the meeting would begin in twenty minutes.

Running out of steam, Nedra slowed her pace. "I feel like I have let so many people down...my girls, my friends, my brother, and you. I'm so very sorry and painfully ashamed." She hung her head and hid her face.

Softly placing a hand on her cheek he said, "Would you like to go home? We don't have to be here, you know. Two people less isn't going to make a difference in the outcome."

Inhaling a long deep breath she said, "I should make an

appearance for the sake of Phree and the retreat. Let's stay to the back of the room and we can leave if necessary."

"That sounds like a good plan, Ned. But listen, when we get back to your house we're going to have a sit-down and I'm going to help you remember how wonderful you are and just how many people love you—not for what you do, but for who you are."

Chapter 25
Brian

Thank goodness whoever was in charge of this meeting had the good sense to change the venue from the little town hall meeting room to the auditorium of Whitney High School. The school campus allowed for ample seating and plenty of parking. Supporters for individual landowners had clustered together, most of them in groups ranging between twenty to thirty people. And then there were the enthusiasts for the Mayflower Quilters Retreat easily numbering over a hundred. The auditorium began to buzz with a rumor that the famous local retreat was bringing in busloads of people.

Flyers stating the evening's agenda were handed out at the door by high school students from Mr. Melton's senior civics class. On stage were several vacant chairs placed in a semicircle for a panel of speakers. An easel held a large computerized map with three different colored lines crossing horizontally over the diagram. In the event things turned ugly, two police officers lingered as inconspicuously as possible along the back wall of the gym.

At five minutes after seven, when it appeared that most people had taken a seat and settled down, the first speaker came to the microphone and said, "Thank you all for coming to this public meeting tonight regarding the I-80 bypass."

Several in the crowd made various displeased grunts and one man said loud enough to be heard, "As if we have any choice in the matter." This caused a ripple of nervous chuckles throughout the room.

Ignoring the outburst, the speaker introduced himself as John Harper, a representative from the Illinois Department of Transportation, or IDOT. "With me tonight to help with our discussion and answer questions are..." He turned and pointed at various people and called out their names and affiliations. "...And finally, this is Winifred Anderson with the FHWA, the Federal Highway Administration."

"In short, our purpose tonight is to provide information on the constitutional authority known as eminent domain, to seize property for the good of the public, and to give everyone here a venue where they can express grievances and ask questions. Our intent is to have this be a fair process making certain that all legal requirements are met."

Five minutes of legal mumbo jumbo followed and then Mr. Harper stepped up to the map. Indicating a line with a laser pointer, he said, "This blue line represents the current route of Interstate 80, typically known as I-80. It runs east-west across the country. Right here..." The red light shined on the southernmost tip of Lake Michigan. "Right here," he repeated, "is where congestion is the worst."

Someone called out, "Too damned bad. That's not our problem."

The speaker continued without acknowledging the interruption. Pointing to a red line he said, "This is our proposed route for the I-80 bypass, the route that affects you as landowners. It will run about fifteen miles south of I-80, and will stretch approximately thirty-five miles long." John Harper stepped back to the podium.

Again, he was interrupted by the same man. "What's that yaller line for?"

"That has nothing to do with this proposal," the speaker said. "Now, I'd like to discuss what..."

The man stood. "If it's got nothin' to do with the proposal, then why is there a yaller line up there?"

"It's um...it's for something entirely different, sir. It shouldn't even be on this map tonight. Someone made a mistake."

"Yer dern right someone made a mistake," the man

said. "I've heard rumors that there's another route planned about a mile south from that red line up there. I'm guessin' that yaller line is near about a mile from that red line. So I'm gonna ask you one more time, mister...what's that yaller line for?"

The attorney onstage stood and came forward. "The yellow line represents a contingency plan in the event that the first proposal doesn't come to fruition."

"Oh, I see," said the man in the audience. "Well, in that case..." He shrugged and made as though he was about to sit down, then he straightened. "And by contingency plan you mean a different proposal. Am I correct?"

"Yes, sir."

"Ma'am, did you really think by throwin' around big words like contingency and fruition that none of us hicks would be able to understand what you're talkin' about?"

The attorney shook her head. "Not at all, sir."

"Then please explain the yaller line *contingency*, because if the people in this room have anathin' to say about it, there's no way that red line proposal will ever come to *fruition*."

The room filled with applause, whistles, and whoops as the rabble-rouser sat down in his seat. Brian whispered to Phree, "That guy just made my job a whole lot easier."

It was clear that the group onstage was confounded with what had happened. Brian felt sure the panel must deal with these types of surprises all the time...*but do they? How often does eminent domain occur in Illinois?*

Harper waited for silence from the crowd before he proceeded to explain the contingency plan. "Yes, Proposal 2 follows the yellow line." Using the laser, the speaker pointed to the notorious yellow line. "Unfortunately, an additional seven bridges will be needed to complete Prop 2 which would incur an astronomical cost. In the best interest of the taxpayers of Illinois, it was deemed to be too expensive. So, Prop 2 was scrubbed."

"That's a pile of bull," Brian said to Phree. "This is where I'm going to get them." He reached to squeeze her hand. "We can do this."

The meeting was now filled with mind-numbing double-talking legalese and droned on for another twenty minutes. Brian noticed people yawning, starting to fidget, and looking at watches, cellphones, and the wall clock. Just when he feared the panel had succeeded in their attempt to make the meeting last so long that comments would be limited, Harper moved to the section where the landowners might have a toehold.

"Number Four," read Mr. Harper. "This proposal and its location have been specifically chosen as to be most beneficial for the greatest good of the public, yet with the least private grievances."

Brian knew they would not let him talk right now, but he stood anyway. "Excuse me, sir," he said in his booming courtroom voice. "I'm Brian Barber and I represent the interests of Phreedom Eaton, owner of the Mayflower Quilters Retreat. I would like to comment on Number Four." Their large contingency of supporters became animated and applauded vigorously. Marge let loose with a few of her legendary earsplitting whistles.

When the noise had died down, Harper told him that they were obligated to finish the meeting before they could field any personal comments or questions.

Brian palmed his hand toward the man who had sparked a revolt over the 'yaller' line on the map. "I didn't realize we were following a protocol tonight," he said. "I have an important point to make just like our friend over there." Mr. Yaller Line smiled broadly and nodded his head.

"You'll have your minute to speak, Mr. Barber, as soon as we're finished with the details of the proposal."

"Excuse me, Mr. Harper. Did you say a minute?" Brian

exaggerated an astonished look on his face.

"Yes sir, the meeting is going long and I'm sure everyone would like to get home soon."

"That's funny," Brian said, "Because I'm sure everyone doesn't care how long it takes to get home. Rather they all prefer that Proposal One be cancelled and replaced with Proposal Two."

The audience thundered its approval of Brian's statement. An exasperated Mr. Harper closed his eyes and then puffed out his cheeks. When the auditorium became quiet again, Brian, still standing, said, "Shall I continue?"

"No, Mr. Barber, you shall not!"

Boos erupted, followed by chants of, 'Let him talk!'

A blatant eye roll by Mr. Harper could be seen all the way in the back of the room. Shouting into the microphone, he warned, "Alright then. Please proceed, Mr. Barber. One minute."

Brian spread his hands out, palms up, in front of him at the same time he shrugged his shoulders and asked, "Seriously, Mr. Harper, the future of the business which I represent, along with the homes and farms of the good people in this auditorium are only worth one minute of your time?"

The deafening chants of, "Let him talk!" came from an angry audience.

Brian kept a morose yet innocent look on his face but inside of that big body, he had his head thrown back and was bursting with laughter. He never thought the scenario he had planned would go this well.

"I will waive the one-minute rule for you, Mr. Barber, as long as you are concise. Now *please* proceed."

"Mr. Harper and our illustrious panel, I will agree with the first part of Number Four under the section *Evidence in support of Resolution of Necessity,* that the I-80 bypass *is* most beneficial for the greatest good of the public. There is no denying that statement. Anyone who has ever had the opportunity…or dare I say, the misfortune to drive that roadway would easily reach the same conclusion.

"I do not, however, agree with the second part of that statement. Prop 1 does not have less private grievances, which is clearly evidenced by the number of people here tonight. On the contrary, Prop 2 holds the least private grievances for the folks in this room. By using your own formula, sir, Prop 1 does NOT meet the legal conditions stated in Number Four under the section, *Evidence in support of Resolution of Necessity*, but Prop 2 *does*, sir, meet them both.

"Therefore, Mr. Harper and our panel of experts, Prop 1 cannot *legally* be permitted to rule over Prop 2. Rather, I respectfully request that Prop 2…also known as the 'yaller line'…be implemented in place of Prop 1."

It didn't take Brian more than two minutes to bring down the house.

Chapter 26
Lettie

Lettie had arrived early to the public meeting on the first shuttle bus from the retreat. Marge wanted to make sure that everyone from the MQR reached the meeting on time. She didn't want anyone from the retreat to make a scene entering the auditorium late. Lettie had been tasked with looking after ninety-eight-year-old Irma and her entourage who were also on the first shuttle.

"Irma is very independent, so don't let her think for a minute that you're her guardian angel for the night," Marge ordered. "I also suggested to her that it might be a good idea if she used the transport wheelchair. After I explained the size of the high school and how far away the auditorium was from the front door, she easily agreed."

Lettie steered her charges to their seats and returned to the door to help with the next shuttle bus of quilters. As she peered out the glass, with arms crossed against the cold, someone tapped her on the shoulder. In the nanosecond before she turned around, Lettie feared that something was wrong with Irma. To her surprise it was Rob McKinnon.

They exchanged an appropriate 'public hug.' "What are you doing here?" Lettie said.

"I was about to ask you the same thing," he said.

Together, they both answered, "I'm here for the public meeting."

"From the map that was sent along with the notice, I wouldn't have thought your property was in danger," Rob said.

"Thank goodness it's not, but the retreat is." Lettie held up her thumb and forefinger an inch apart. "The bypass is slated to run within inches of the building. How about you?"

"Our property is smack on the firing line," he said. "It's scaring the heck out of me. I can't begin to imagine packing up, moving, and finding a new place."

"Oh no, Rob," Lettie said. "I'm so sorry." She touched his arm. "There simply has to be another way. I'm hoping something can be done tonight to sway the committee."

"I'd like to think that's possible, but from what I've learned it's as good as a done deal if it's gotten this far."

"Why didn't you tell me over the weekend?" she asked.

"I didn't want bad news to compete with the relaxed atmosphere we had created," he said. "Besides it was a nice break not to be worrying about it for a while."

"Lettie!" a voice called out.

She twirled to see Helen coming toward her with the next batch of protesting quilters following behind her like a flock of baby ducklings. There was no mistaking the look on Helen's face: What are you doing with the sleigh guy?

"Oh, Helen," she said a little flustered. "Do you remember Rob McKinnon? He drove the sleigh at Nancy's wedding. His property is also in danger. So he came to the meeting tonight just like we did." *I sound like a blathering idiot!* Turning back to Rob she said, "If you're alone, would you like to join our group and sit with us?"

"Yeah, I'd like that," he said.

The looks Lettie received from her friends throughout the evening were epic. Yes, there was some hand-holding, during which Rosa would *not* stop elbowing her from the other side. At one point before the meeting started, Rob left his seat to use the washroom. Lettie was instantly surrounded and pummeled with questions: When did this start? Why haven't you told us about this? And of course there was Rosa's cross-examination starting with: Have you slept with him yet?

Lettie tackled their questions with quick answers and laughed at them. "As they say, I guess the cat's out of the bag."

By ten twenty-five, after comments and questions, the main speaker agreed there needed to be adjustments made to the proposals. The meeting concluded with hope in everyone's heart leaving Brian and Mr. Yaller Line looking like a rock stars.

A group of protesters clustered around Brian. "This isn't over yet," he said, "but I believe we are in better shape than when we walked in here tonight. I'm going to continue pushing and fighting until they're sick of me. We need to keep the heat turned up on these people with emails and letters. I'll post the appropriate names with addresses on my website, as will the MQR. Stay active. My gut tells me that we'll hear from them soon if it's good news; otherwise this could take some time while they prepare their next attack."

The group disbursed and Marge made her way through the crowd to be introduced to Rob. After a brief exchange of pleasantries, Marge said, "Thanks for your help tonight, Lettie, but we can take it from here. Half the quilters are tired and will go straight to bed once we return to the retreat." She winked at Lettie in a way that Rob couldn't see.

Lettie knew that Marge had let her off the hook so she could leave with Rob if she chose to. She asked him, "Feel like a late night? We'll have to swing by the retreat and pick up my truck."

"Absolutely," he answered. "Maggie's companion can stay as long as needed. They're probably both asleep by now."

"And I've got the neighbor kid checking in on Picasso tonight. Not knowing how long the meeting would take, I wanted to make sure he could get outside if he needed."

Leaving the auditorium, Lettie noticed Sunnie sitting next to a haggard looking Phree who was nearly catatonic. Where the heck was Nedra tonight anyway? Lettie had something she wanted to talk to her about.

On their way to the MQR to retrieve Lettie's truck, Rob said, "I'm starved. How about you?"

"Famished," Lettie told him. "I didn't get a chance to eat dinner before the meeting. Any idea where we can go this late at night?"

"How are you with a big juicy bar burger?" he asked. "There's a place a few miles down the road off the beaten path that has the best."

"Are we talking about Phil's Place?" asked Lettie.

"The one and only." Pulling onto the retreat's long driveway, Rob said, "Since everyone around here knows where Phil's is, you lead the way and I'll follow you."

With the large retreat building looming ahead, she asked, "Would you and Maggie like a tour of the MQR someday? I'd like to show it to both of you. I think Maggie would especially enjoy it."

"I can definitely speak for my sister when I say we'd both love a tour." Rob maneuvered his car next to Lettie's truck in the employee lot. "She was bugging me to get inside of the building when we were here on the wedding day."

"Let's make it happen soon," she said as she opened the car door. Rob started to get out of the car, but she told him, "Stay there. I can practically jump in my car without my feet even touching the ground."

As the key triggered the engine to start, Lettie rubbed her gloved hands together for warmth. Many of the lights were still on inside the retreat. She was willing to bet that Chef Evelyn had whipped up a late night treat for the hungry protesters. With adrenaline running high from the public meeting and an additional kick from sugar, it was sure to be a long and most likely boisterous night at the MQR.

Occasionally glancing in the rearview mirror to verify that Rob was still behind her, she caught herself being happy...really happy that this man was in her life.

"So, what would you do?" Lettie wadded up her paper napkin and plopped it onto her empty plate. "By the way…incredible burger."

"*If* those really are the kids that hurt Picasso and damaged your car, then in my opinion they need to be held accountable. And by accountable I mean more than a slap on the wrist."

"Brian explained to me that Illinois animal cruelty law is considered to be the model for other states to follow. He also said that in all fifty states, animal cruelty is now a felony."

"Do we know if these kids are juveniles?" Rob asked.

"I don't know their ages but if they're in the final year of high school, there's a possibility that they might be."

"They could still be close enough to eighteen to be tried as an adult."

"I've thought about it a lot, Rob. I've weighed the impact a sentence might have on their lives but I can't let this slide…especially what they did to Picasso. I won't deny that part of me wants revenge, but more than that I want to do the right thing."

Rob placed a hand over hers and said, "I'd personally want to wring their necks."

"Spoken like a man," she told him.

The warmth she felt from his calloused palm spread through her body at an alarming rate. They intertwined fingers.

"From what you've told me, the decision is out of your hands. The state will prosecute whether you want to or not. Maybe that's a blessing." He gently squeezed her hand. "It sounds like you won't have to make that decision. Besides," he said, "a conviction could save countless animals from abuse in the future if it helps to get these kids on track."

Lettie puffed air from deep in her lungs. "That's true. I only hope this was the stupidity of youth and not a lifelong pattern." Shaking her head, Lettie said, "I will never live long enough to understand animal cruelty."

"That makes two of us," Rob said, then added, "That goes for cruelty of any kind."

Lettie covered her mouth with her free hand to stifle a yawn. "I don't know about you, but that burger made me tired."

"What's on tap for tomorrow?" Rob asked as they rose. Lettie wrapped an infinity scarf around her neck.

"I've got to get in the studio and start on a new series of quilts I've been sketching out. The last few weeks have been crazy and I admit that I've been rather neglectful in the creative department." They both buttoned their coats and Lettie slipped on a pair of leather gloves. "How about you?"

"The usual, I suppose. I'll oversee the body shop and keep an eye on Mags who cares for the animals every day." Rob held his keys in his hand and studied them for a moment. "Are you still okay with me picking up the Mustang in the afternoon?" Raising his hand as though taking a pledge, he said, "I promise that car will leave your garage tomorrow, no more using it for an excuse to see you." He smiled a shy, handsome smile.

She smacked his arm and smiled back at this good-looking man. "News flash, buddy, you don't need an excuse to see me."

They left a tip, shared the cost of the burgers at the register, and headed arm in arm for their vehicles without a word. Their warm breath hung in the air for a split second as it hit the cold night.

"Are you sure you don't want me to follow you home?" he asked.

"That's kind of you, but you'd have to double back," she said. "I'll be fine, I'm used to being on my own."

"I guess we're going to have to remedy that," Rob said, and sealed the deal with a goodnight kiss.

Chapter 27
Nedra

The steel-gray winter's sky hadn't changed in hours except for a few thin clouds that occasionally scudded across it. Birds flitted to the feeders with hopes that life-giving seeds had finally refilled the numerous empty feeders. Most flew away immediately while others lingered on the ground, scratching for an overlooked morsel. The sound of the trash collector's truck lumbered down the road, brakes squeaking at every stop. Nedra's garbage receptacle still sat gaping open and overflowing at the side of the garage. Trash inside the kitchen spilled over the full container and left a nasty smell.

Nedra sipped a near empty cold cup of coffee. A junco flicked the grass with both feet, working vigorously to turn up a treasure of seeds to help it survive another day. The little gray and white bird had worked so hard for that scrap of food. She felt she had something in common with that determined bird: They were both hard workers and trusted that their tomorrows would be the same as yesterday.

Another sip of cold coffee.

How long? How long would it take to be a kindred spirit of that bird again? Would she ever be excited for another day or would they all be lonely and depressing reminders of things she had lost?

What am I going to do with myself?

The only reason Nedra rose from the kitchen table was to use the washroom. She had to admit that it felt better to move around. She had to further confess that, even though she didn't feel like it, she *should* be working on the MQR's social media sites. They needed updating after last night's meeting, along with a 'call to action' for an enthusiastic letter-writing campaign.

Enough of feeling sorry for myself. I'm going to scare everyone away if I'm not careful.

With a momentous effort, Nedra put one step in front of the other to get herself upstairs.

The hot water in the shower began to feel lukewarm. It was ten forty-five in the morning, long past time to dry off and start the day over. Each step, every movement, brought her out of the abyss of sadness a little bit more. It was going to take a while—probably a long while, but she would show those self-centered cheats at *Excel* that they had made a mistake when they let her go. She needed to remind herself that the severance package they offered her really was incredible. By being frugal it should last a few years.

All in all, as she liked to remind herself, things could be worse.

By the time she chose a winter white mohair cowl neck sweater that looked stunning against her dark skin, paired it with crisply pressed jeans, and knee-high mahogany colored leather boots, Nedra Lange was on her game again...well, not quite but almost. She simply had to make it through this first long day.

One of the three cameras Nedra placed on her desk at the MQR desperately needed to be charged. Removing the correct charger from her purse and unwinding it, she answered Marge's question as convincingly as possible. "I'm feeling better today. Being here helps." Plugging the charger into the camera, she added, "As the dust was settling around me this morning, I realized that I still had a job at the retreat. A job which I like very much and one that I have ignored for the past few days."

Marge came close and rested a gentle hand on Nedra's arm. "Everyone would understand if you need to regroup for a while."

"That's kind, Marge, but that's not what's going to help me. Having a purpose, enjoying what I'm doing, and building something new is what will keep me sane."

"You go, girl," Marge said. "If you need anything let us know — remember we've all got your back."

"Bring me up to speed on the passengers." Part of the tradition of the Mayflower Quilters Retreat was to maintain the fantasy at all times that their guests were passengers on a twenty-first-century version of the *Mayflower*. "Is there anything or anyone I should focus on?"

Nedra took notes and asked questions while Marge talked. Twenty minutes later she was armed with information. By way of a light step and a renewed purpose, she headed toward the Brewster Quilting Room where she could prove to herself that she was a survivor.

Approaching the large community room she felt uneasy as she associated the hallway with the place where she had received the bad news about her career. Heat filled her and a light sweat formed as she passed the exact spot that Samantha what's-her-name said the words: Your services will no longer be required. Holding her chin up, she continued walking. *They will not break me. I'll show them that there are wonderful things ahead for Nedra Lange.*

The energy, sound, and joy in the room were tangible. Nedra felt the dynamic energy of movement — it was all around her. From the smallest rhythm of feeding fabric through a sewing machine, reaching for another piece, and then repeating the process; to hefting a nearly finished queen-sized quilt to an ironing station; to billowing out a pieced top and placing it on the floor for inspection — the room was energetic.

It was a rare moment when the whirring of a sewing machine could not be heard. But the heartbeat of this room was the sound of voices — women making new friends, quietly sharing hopeful or sad moments, involved with on-the-spot tutorials, giggles, or raucous laughter. This gathering of conflicting noises was a symphony to a quilter.

Joy reigned simply for those who were fortunate enough to be here. Smiles were fixed features on most everyone's face. Nedra knew from experience that handing out and accepting compliments on work, boosts the spirits of both the giver and receiver. Quilt making among other women had always been healing and beneficial to her soul.

This, indeed, is a magical place.

I am fortunate to be part of it.

Starting at one side of the room, the side farthest from the treat center, Nedra stood back and studied one of the quilters that Marge had told her about. Robyn was about half finished piecing a magnificent Double Wedding Ring quilt top. She had chosen a palette of black and white which was unusual for a DWR, but proved to be absolutely stunning.

"I'm making this for my son and future daughter-in-law," she told Nedra.

"When's the wedding?" Nedra asked. As she clicked one photo after another of the work in progress and the quilter, it crossed her mind that Robyn was awfully young to have a son getting married.

"It's undetermined at this point," Robyn laughed. "Cooper is only four years old. I'm making this and carefully packing it away for the big day. That way I won't have to stress over finishing it on time."

"That's actually a great idea. I should do that for my daughters," Nedra told her. "I have to admit that it's nice to meet someone who is way more organized and anal than I am...and I mean that in the nicest way."

The women shared a laugh and Nedra said, "Would you mind emailing me a photo of this beauty when it's finished?" Nedra handed a card containing her contact information to Robyn.

At the next station was a newbie quilter. Kalina was a friend of Robyn's who quickly became hooked on what she called her new hobby.

"I was making a simple Nine Patch quilt. Robyn told me it was a good place to start, so I made a stack of these things." She fanned through the pile of pieced fabric as though they were a stack of playing cards. "On Pinterest late one night, I saw a photo of something called a Disappearing Nine Patch, then another, and another. My heart started racing and I couldn't wait to cut into some of these blocks to see what I had." She reached for a different pile of quilt blocks and started to spread them out on her table. "This is what they look like now. I love them."

"They're wonderful." Nedra praised her as she examined a block close up. "There's nothing like your first quilt. You should be very proud for pushing the envelope and trying this. Most people wouldn't have the courage to cut up their first quilt blocks simply to experiment."

Kalina beamed. "This is the most fun I've had in a long time. Robyn and I are already talking about coming back next year."

"When you do, be sure to bring the finished quilt with you," Nedra said.

No one was 'home' at some of the stations, but evidence of occupancy showed with all of the flotsam and jetsam surrounding the areas. Many women napped in the afternoon so they could stay up later at night, some people were doing hand stitching on the sofas, and there were always quilters huddled around the treat center grazing on snacks. Nedra stopped at each station where a quilter sat and learned about the quilt in progress as well as the person.

Heading toward the next quilter, a fragment of an idea drifted through Nedra's mind. It was a flimsy filament that she couldn't quite grasp. By the time she came face-to-face with Irma, also known as their eldest passenger, the thought had disappeared from her mind. Nedra pulled up an unused chair and the two women began to talk. Irma never lost the slow rhythm of her pace as she continued to sew and tell her story.

She started out almost apologetically by saying, "I used to hand sew most of my quilts and I admit to being a bit of a snob about that. I thought if it wasn't done by hand then it wasn't done right. But when my arthritis got so bad I had to make a choice." Another piece of fabric was sent beneath the needle of her machine. "The bottom line was: I could stick to my stubborn rules about quilting and give up sewing altogether, or I could accept the challenge and use a sewing machine to do what my hands could no longer accomplish."

Irma waited a moment and when Nedra didn't say anything, she continued her story. "I chose to never give up. If something is taken away from you, especially something you hold very dear, you've got to find a way to keep going. Be proud and happy that you conquered the challenge."

It was as if Irma spoke directly to Nedra's own situation. The tenacity of this woman was inspirational and she, Nedra Lange, would draw on that motivation to make the changes needed to keep going and stay happy.

The stitching family of Irma Flynn surrounded their matriarch. They sewed, talked, and added comments as Nedra listened and took notes about the life of this amazing woman.

Forty minutes later, with page after page of notes about Irma's story hand written on a pad of paper, Nedra smiled politely at the rest of the quilters in the Brewster Room, stopping to chat with a few. The thread of a thought that had appeared in her mind earlier had returned as a full-blown idea.

She had the beginning of an idea about how she would proceed with her life.

Chapter 28
Lettie

Picasso hobbled alongside his person as they walked from the house to the studio barn. He stopped to lift his leg on one of the snowbanks created by the plow and left a patch of the much dreaded 'yellow snow.' He proceeded to halt their progress several times to sniff out possible dangers around the parking area. Waiting patiently for her buddy to smell his way to the studio, Lettie knew the fresh air and excitement of this simple outing would tire him out quickly.

Once inside the warmth of the studio, her favorite old man limped his way to the doggie bed, and finding just the right spot in which to collapse, he did so with a contented snuffle.

Eager to continue the little bit of progress she had made on her quilt designs, Lettie picked up where she left off the first time that Rob and Maggie had come for the Mustang. Resting near the green cutting mat was a stack of two-and-a-half-inch squares of various colors and patterns. She planned on making this first quilt with a more 'scrappy' approach. Her design called for twenty-five of the same two-and-a-half-inch miniature blocks sewn together to end up with a larger block that would measure a finished size of ten inches. She decided to make one finished block so she could see if her measurements were correct and to get an idea of how the quilt would look. Lettie chose the easiest design first.

In her mind, she visualized simply whipping up these mini-blocks and sewing them together, but she knew it would require more time than that...much more time. After all, there was no rush. Her scheme of producing a quilt pattern book for this series would end up being a long-haul project of epic proportions — that is if it were ever to become a reality.

Creative motivation was what drove this project for Lettie. She was excited to her core and couldn't stop imagining the fun of the countless layouts this quilt pattern would offer. She'd need to find a pattern writer. While she was generally good with organization, one thing for sure was that her mind didn't work in the way needed to write a quilt pattern. Several years ago Lettie had given pattern writing a whirl with another of her designs which she thought might be marketable. She was useless at the task, and the prototype of the quilt along with her failed instructions were tucked away on a shelf somewhere deep in her studio.

Attempting a project of this magnitude did not frighten Lettie. Other than her love life, Lettie was not afraid of failure. She had read somewhere that creative people were risk takers who didn't have the same filter for failure as most people do. It sure seemed to apply to her in the artistic sense — it was easy for her to dream big and move forward with a plan that many would never consider. Publishing a quilt book of her designs…was she crazy? But once the idea had formed, she could no more turn back than jump from a speeding train.

If only some of that boldness could rub off and give her the strength she needed to move forward with Rob. She was growing very fond of him and it scared the daylights out of her. Would it work itself out with time and a lot of baby steps? Should she jump in with both feet and be the fearless woman she was when it came to creativity? Thinking of Rob as her sewing machine whirred and her iron steamed made solving her age-old dilemma seem promising.

And then it hit her…Rob wasn't the problem. After all these years of pushing men away and blaming all of them, it was time that she took some of the responsibility. *She* had chosen badly; *she* had picked a loser. Maybe she had finally learned from her mistake. And just maybe Rob was the solution.

The sound of dogs barking came from deep within her tote bag. Nestled somewhere between snacks, fabric, and quilting magazines, her cell phone rang. When she finally retrieved the device, she saw Brian's picture on the screen.

"Hey there," she answered. "What's up?"

"I've got some news about those three teens."

Taking a seat in the nearest chair, she said, "And?"

"It's them."

Lettie felt as if someone sat on her chest; her heart thumped heavy and hard. She waited for Brian to continue.

"The police brought them in and kept them separated...two boys and a girl."

"What?" Lettie was thunderstruck. "Did you say one of them is a girl?"

"Yeah, and from what I've heard, she's one tough cookie. The boys broke down and cried, but the girl..." Brian paused for a beat. "That girl never once flinched. She never showed any remorse."

Under her breath, Lettie said, "What in the heck is wrong with people nowadays?"

Continuing, Brian told her, "Two of them have already turned eighteen and one is underage by a few months so a parent had to be with him for questioning. From what I understand they all denied any knowledge of the incident, but at some point one of them cracked and ratted out the other two. That started a chain reaction and they all squealed."

Lettie reached for the tote and grabbed a brown lunch sack. Spilling the contents onto the floor, she began to breathe into the bag.

"Are you okay?" Brian asked.

Pulling the bag from her mouth she said, "I'm fine."

"The long and the short of it is that they have all been taken into custody and the underage boy is being transported to a juvenile facility. At that point, none of them had lawyered up, but I suspect that's changed by now. Grand theft auto and animal abuse are not to be taken lightly."

Once again, tears pooled in Lettie's eyes. "Do we know why they targeted my Mustang?"

"Apparently the boys saw you driving home from the retreat the morning after Nancy's wedding. They followed at a distance and when you turned into your driveway they drove past with plans to come back in a few days." Brian sighed. "Without any thought to the trouble they could get into, they said that they simply wanted to drive around in a cool car. Like most teens, I'm sure they never expected to get caught."

Lettie had to choke out the next words. "Which one hurt Picasso?"

Brian cleared his throat. "I'm shocked by this and sorry to be the one that tells you Lettie, but it was the girl."

After a sharp intake of breath, Lettie said nothing. She found it repulsive that someone of her own sex could be so abusive toward a helpless animal. *Cruelty clearly knows no gender and neither does stupidity.*

"What happens next?" she asked.

"Just like we talked about, the State of Illinois will prosecute so you don't have to worry about pressing charges. You'll most likely have to appear in court and swear under oath that you didn't give any of them permission to drive your car. That's standard."

"I'll gladly testify," Lettie said.

"There's one more thing."

Lettie's blood ran cold at the tone in Brian's voice.

He cleared his throat. "I'm warning you, Lettie, this will not be easy for you to hear."

"Go ahead."

"The juvenile took a video on his cell phone of the female beating Picasso."

Light-headed, Lettie positioned her head between her legs as she held onto the phone. "That little bastard didn't lift a finger to help my dog, yet somehow thought it would be fun to take a video of someone beating him?"

"That's not all," Brian said. "He allegedly posted the video on YouTube."

Lettie dropped to her knees in front of her sleeping dog, embraced him, and wept.

Chapter 29
Nedra

As Nedra shrugged on her coat, Marge asked, "Wanna stay for dinner at the retreat tonight?"

"That sounds wonderful, but I need to get home." Fastening the buttons, Nedra said, "Just so you know, I've been tweeting all day about the public meeting and the letter-writing campaign."

"I got a few notifications earlier from Twitter and saw some of your tweets. Good job," Marge said.

"I also hit Facebook, Instagram, and Pinterest with some posts. You never know who might see them and be compelled to join our fight to keep the retreat alive."

"You're our very own social media guru," Marge said. "You do realize, don't you, that none of us would be half as good as you are with all that stuff."

Marge was the kindhearted cheerleader of the group and Nedra knew she was trying to lift her spirits with a compliment about her work. Smiling, she said, "Aw, thanks Marge, you're the best."

"I only speak the truth," Marge told her.

Wanting to get home where she could lose herself in some hand sewing, Nedra edged closer to the door. "I posted information at the top of the blog concerning the letter-writing campaign. It's a fixed spot so it won't change position as I blog about the retreat...which I did today, so we're all caught up with our communications." With her hand on the doorknob, she added, "There's a nice piece on some of the quilters and, of course, I highlighted Irma. She's been through a lot. She's quite a woman...she's a real warrior."

"What a great description," Marge said.

"I've been thinking that most quilters are warriors of some kind or another." Nedra's pulse picked up. "We keep creating no matter what happens in our life. Quilting is not simply *in* our blood...quilting *is* our blood. It feeds us, it sustains us, and it weathers all.

Nedra knew she would write a book and without even starting the first page, she knew exactly what the title would be.

This whole mess is going to work out after all.

While driving home, Nedra envisioned the look on the faces of the three corporate creeps that had fired her, when they found out that she had written a best-selling book. She knew it was a silly, immature thought but nonetheless it made her feel good right now. Sweet revenge. The truth was that most likely those soulless ghouls had not given her a second thought since sending her packing the other day.

Her daydream of getting revenge was interrupted as her cell phone rang. She pushed the button on the Bluetooth earpiece. Without thinking and out of sheer habit from her days at *Excel*, she said, "Nedra Lange."

There was silence on the other end. She tried again. "Hello? Can I help you?"

A shaky voice said, "I hope so."

"With whom am I speaking?"

"You always were so proper and polite. I never would have guessed that you had it in you."

Nedra pulled her car into a Walgreen's. She was trembling as she asked again...this time fearing the answer. "I'm sorry, but who is this?"

"Don't you recognize my voice, Nedra? It's Sheila...Sheila Haynes. Don's widow. And I think we need to talk."

"Oh my God, Brian! What am I going to do? Don's wife, I mean widow called me two minutes ago. She wants to get together and talk. I think I'm going to have a heart attack."

"Slow down. You're going to be fine." Brian was using his calming voice but it wasn't working. "Remember, you haven't done anything wrong. You were simply helping a friend in a sticky situation."

That set her off. "A sticky situation?" She heard her voice go high and shrill. "He had a...a...rabid affair with another woman and they had a child together. To you that's nothing more than a sticky situation?"

"Nedra, I'm not the enemy here. You're going to blow a gasket if you don't calm down." His voice was firm, verging on anger. "Tell me exactly what she said."

"Nothing. She said nothing." Unwilling and unable to drive her car, she stayed in the Walgreen's parking lot shouting into her phone like a crazy person. "She identified herself and said that we needed to talk. That's it."

"Did she mention where she wanted to get together?"

"She wants to meet at the Starbucks by the *Excel* building tomorrow at ten in the morning."

Brian roared a disbelieving laugh. "A Starbucks...how covert. Couldn't she come up with something more original than that?"

"I don't care where we meet. I want to get this over with and soon. After what I've been through these past few days, I don't need Don's drama and dark secrets in my life anymore."

"Atta girl," Brian said softly. "Now we're getting somewhere. You need to purge this nonsense from your conscience and hand it off to his wife. I'll go with you to the meeting at Starbucks tomorrow. Call me when you get home and we'll figure out the details."

After several moments of diaphragmatic breathing techniques, she put her car in gear and pulled away from Walgreen's. Nedra felt angry at her ex-boss for dragging her into this mess by placing her squarely between his wife and his mistress—and angry at herself for allowing it to happen. Boiling with emotions, she selfishly added ...*And if it wasn't for him dying...I'd still have a job!*

Chapter 30
Lettie

The familiar reverberation from the McKinnons' tow truck reached Picasso's alert ears as the wrecker lumbered down the lane. Associating the sound with a visit from his friend, the shepherd limped to the door and whined. Lettie assumed he had to go out to do his business. Grabbing her coat to accompany him, she finally heard the rumbling engine for herself. Associating the sound with a visit from Rob, she opened the door and both of them left the studio with anticipation.

The passenger door of the rig opened and Maggie exited from the cab with practiced caution. With feet firmly on the ground and wide smile, she spread her arms out to her sides, and called in the thick-tongued way that Lettie had come to love, "Picasso." The shepherd did a four-legged version of a quickstep-limp and greeted his new pal with tail wags and doggie kisses.

Once again, Lettie's heart expanded in her chest at the sight of Maggie. She was quickly growing to feel a strong connection to this kindhearted woman and her brother.

The tow truck was backed into the area in front of the garage and Rob was busy with winches or chains or whatever they were. He looked up from his work. "Today we do this for sure." He tugged on a cable of some sort. "We're gonna get your baby on the flatbed and on its way to the body shop."

Lettie strode to where he was and after they each took a furtive glance at Maggie's back, they stole a kiss. "I'm glad to see you," she said.

He held her at arm's length and locked onto her eyes with his. "Not nearly as happy as I am to see you," he told her. A flicker of a look over Lettie's shoulder toward Maggie, and a slightly longer kiss was shared between the two of them. "I'd hate to interrupt this greeting with such a silly question..." Rob paused with mischief in his eyes. "Could you please open the garage door?"

Swatting his arm and laughing, Lettie said, "How romantic of you."

She tapped the code into the key pad and the door rose slowly. This was the first time Rob had seen the damage to the Mustang in daylight and he whistled long and low. "Holy cow, looks like those creeps really did a number on this old gal, and in such a short distance. Thank goodness they didn't get onto the county road with her." He ran a hand over a fender and bent for a closer look. When he stood, he lightly thumped the hood and said, "Yep. We can fix 'er up as good as new for you."

"You McKinnons are real superheroes," Lettie said. "You're about to breathe life back into my crumpled car, and at the same time your sister is helping heal my abused dog. Yep, superheroes. That's what you two are...nothing short of superheroes."

Rob kicked at some gravel with the toe of his boot. "Aw shucks, ma'am, you've gone and plum embarrassed me now."

Playing along, Lettie said, "That's what us damsels in distress do, ya know."

Tossing his head back with a laugh, Rob firmly stated, "Leticia, my dear, you are a lot of strong and wonderful things, but let me point out that a damsel in distress is *not* in your wheelhouse."

After much grinding of gears, and a few bangs and thuds, her bruised 1969 Mustang was pulled by a greasy cable and eventually rested on the flatbed of the McKinnons' tow truck. Lettie held Picasso's collar on one side and Maggie helped by holding the other side. They watched as Rob was all motion. The leap from the cab to the ground happened in one long movement and several trips from the cab to the back of the bed were achieved in a matter of minutes. All of the paraphernalia was gathered, wound up, and then stored out of sight ready for the next time it was needed.

No wonder he's in good shape. He never stops moving.

Brushing his hands together and then swiping them on his jeans, he joined the gawking bystanders, saying, "She's on her way to being whole again." He bent to rub Picasso's head and ears. When he stood, he added, "Well, come on Mags, we need to leave Lettie alone so she can get her work done."

This was met with an unhappy moan and an extended lower lip. "Do we have to?" Looking toward Lettie, she asked, "Can we stay?"

"Remember, Mags, I told you that we were coming here only to pick up Lettie's car today." He patted Maggie on the shoulder.

"But you said that the last two times we came here, too." Maggie crossed her arms over her chest and continued pouting.

"She's got you there," Lettie said. Not wanting to interfere, she tentatively said, "Unless you have other chores that need to be done, maybe you'd like to visit for a while..." She let the sentence trail off.

Maggie started her excited tippy toe dance. "Yes, yes. Oh, say yes, Rob. Please."

Rob looked from his sister to Lettie.

"I have homemade vegetable beef soup cooking in the Crock Pot." Lettie pretended to be timid. "That is if you might be hungry for some dinner."

"That does it." Rob threw his hands in the air. "We're staying."

Maggie had to reach high to fling her arms around Lettie's neck. "I love being with you, Miss Lettie."

Their routine was well established: dinner, UNO,

Maggie falls asleep by Picasso, and Lettie and Rob talk and smooch by the fireplace. Lettie loved the cozy closeness of sharing her life with these two people. It felt like family.

"I didn't want to talk about this in front of Maggie." Lettie felt Rob stiffen next to her and she realized that he was fearful of bad news about their relationship after she had just warned him the other night that she was afraid to let someone into her life. Lettie placed a comforting hand on his knee and said, "It's not about us." Rob relaxed immediately. It was time for Lettie to be strong and take a giant leap. "I like us. I like all of us together…a lot."

He held her face in the palm of his hand. "If you haven't noticed, I like us too." He placed a short kiss on her mouth and then said, "Tell me what's troubling you."

He already knows me well enough to realize that I'm troubled about something and he cares enough to want to know what it is. I may have had to wait a long time for this guy, but at this point I'd say it was worth it.

"I heard from Brian," she said.

He ran a knuckle down the side of her cheek. "Oh, Lettie. Tell me everything."

And she did.

And it felt good and right to share her difficulties with him.

With her beloved Mustang on the flatbed and a sleepy Maggie waiting in the tow truck, the two lovebirds shared a long embrace. "It feels good to be held by you," Lettie said.

"It feels good to hold you, Lettie." He swayed back and forth with her to an unheard rhythm. "I'm smitten, Ms. Peabody. In only a few short days, you've captured my heart."

In a breathless voice, she asked, "Now that you have my car and don't have an excuse to come back, when will I see you again?"

"Tomorrow? The next day? Forever?" he answered. "It's your choice. Whenever you want me, I'm yours."

Lettie did not withdraw to her safe place. It was time for her to finally take a risk.

Chapter 31
Brian

The overnighted white cardboard mailing envelope was sitting front and center on Brian's desk when he arrived at his office. It could be concerning any number of clients, as overnight mail in a law office was not unusual. After checking the return label, he knew that the letter inside could affect many people about whom he cared deeply.

This one was personal.

Hesitating in his leather office chair, Brian prepared himself for the outcome of the eminent domain battle. This had not been a quick reaction; this had been a supersonic fast response. Brian feared an answer that would be something like: too bad, so sad—you lose.

He pinched the little zip tab between his large fingers. With a tug and the sound of thin cardboard ripping a sealed white envelope slipped from the package onto his desktop. Gliding a letter opener under the flap and slicing the paper open, he freed the missive inside and began to read.

A short, concise, and unbendable message came through loud and clear. A conclusion was reached and it was final. Now Brian had to decide the best way to tell Phree and the board members of the Mayflower Quilters Retreat.

But first he had to attend a meeting with his sister at one of the millions of Starbucks in the city of Chicago.

Chapter 32
Nedra

The southern suburbs were enjoying an unusually warm day for the end of January. It was a balmy forty-one degrees and the sunshine that reflected off the snow was painful to the eyes. In contrast, a freezing wind blew off the ice on Lake Michigan as brother and sister walked in the shadows from the towering buildings deep in the city of Chicago. Today was as cold as any other winter day.

Nedra tugged her collar close with one hand as she held a section of her cashmere scarf up to her nose and mouth to keep them warm. Brian grasped her elbow and guided her through the gale that howled among the concrete canyons. Up ahead were the steamy windows of the Starbucks which was located closest to the *Excel* building. She had often visited this very coffee shop over the past many years.

Entering the warmth of the establishment, Nedra checked for Sheila Haynes as she unwound the scarf from her neck. Good, no Sheila yet. They could warm up a bit and regroup from their trek through the cold. A businesswoman rose from a table and Nedra practically lunged for it. Tables could be hard to acquire this time of day, and she sure as heck didn't want to discuss Don's affair with his widow while standing in the corner.

"Good work," Brian said. "You hold the table and I'll get us some coffee. What do you want?"

She absolutely didn't want coffee; her nervous stomach couldn't handle it right now. "Get me a hot chocolate."

"If she gets here before I get back, don't start without me," he said.

"You can count on that," she scoffed. There wasn't a

chance she'd attempt anything but small talk with Don's recent widow. 'Tied in knots' was so cliché, but that was exactly how her stomach felt—one giant tightly tangled knot.

Nedra watched Sheila walk through the doorway. Sheila's eyes flicked over the people at the tables and came to rest on Nedra. *Oh crap. Hurry up, Brian.* Holding Nedra's gaze, she walked past her and headed toward the counter. Apparently Sheila needed some fortification, too.

Brian returned to the table first, and when Sheila came toward them he stood. Holding out her chair, he said, "Permit me to express our condolences on the loss of your husband."

As she sat in the chair and Brian pushed her toward the table, Sheila replied rather curtly, "Thank you, Brian."

"Where would you like to begin?" Brian asked.

Sheila retrieved two folders from her tote bag, with a stack of papers in each folder.

Nedra felt as if her hot chocolate might reappear as her stomach roiled behind her calm façade. Using an old calming trick from her past, Nedra focused on her manicured fingernails.

"To start with, this is not a legal discussion, Nedra. However, if you feel more comfortable with your lawyer present, I have no problem with that."

Nedra nodded her head.

"I also want you to know that this is not a trap. I have my suspicions of what my husband was up to but, woman to woman, I'd like you to help me understand what transpired."

Nedra nodded and fisted her hand over her abdomen under the table.

Sheila continued. "Several years ago I suspected Don was having an affair...or should I say another affair."

Stunned, Nedra knew her face reflected surprise.

"That's right, the man everyone knew as Mr. Family Man and who was hailed as a nice guy was..." Sheila studied the tabletop for a moment. "This is hard for me to admit, but my husband was a philanderer, and one of epic proportions."

Nedra was speechless. Not that she had said much up to this point, but right now she couldn't have spit out a word if she had to. For a moment she wondered if Sheila was making up some elaborate hoax for some reason. But to what end? Finding her voice, Nedra whispered, "I had no idea."

"I can see that you didn't and that's part of the reason I wanted to meet with you face-to-face. I needed to witness your reaction. While it's true you could be lying," Sheila smiled, "I don't think you're that good of an actress."

Nedra returned a smile at the comment. She still didn't understand where this was going, but certainly wanted to find out.

"I will say there were times when I thought you might be one of his 'other' women."

"Me?" Nedra said, incredulous. "Why me?"

"Well, you're beautiful..."

Nedra felt heat rise to her face. It had been a while since she had blushed.

"He spent time with you every day, and he spoke so highly of you. It was as though he was infatuated with you."

"We never...that is, nothing ever happened between us. We had a respectable boss-employee relationship that simply grew into a friendship over the years." Nedra had so many questions she'd like to ask this woman, but knew she'd never have the opportunity to do so.

"Our financial advisor retired several years ago." Sheila said this as she rifled through one of the folders. Finding what she was looking for, she moved the bundle of documents to the front of the stack. "Miranda Barry took over his clients. Upon Don's death, I requested a compilation of our assets. Among them I found this accounting. Miranda undoubtedly was not aware of the backstory connected to this account, and I suspect it was sent to me by accident. It wouldn't have been like Don to have overlooked such a damning detail as sending this document to me upon his death."

Nedra knew what Sheila had before she pulled it from the folder and held it in her hand.

"Who is Baby Kelsey?" she asked. "And why are you in charge of its trust fund?"

"It's a very long story," Nedra said.

"I'll buy a fresh round of coffee for all of us," Shelia said. "Let's get started."

On their way back to the suburbs, Nedra said, "I still can't believe it. Don of all people... I never would have guessed. Never. He played me, Brian. I trusted him and he played me for a fool. I've worried about him, how his wife would react after he died, if I had done the right thing by helping him, and all along this wasn't even his first time." Gritting her teeth she said, "I'm so angry right now I could spit! How ignorant could I be?"

"If it makes you feel any better, I never would have guessed either. Don't be too hard on yourself, Ned. He was a con man and knew exactly how to get what he wanted," Brian said. "Once again it just proves that you never know a person even though you think you do."

"I really feel sorry for Sheila. She says she stayed for the children and then admitted to being just plain stupid. But how does a woman think so little of herself that she'll live with that kind of behavior?"

"There's a lot of reasons a wife might stay with a womanizer, Ned," Brian answered.

"I can't think of a valid one. I mean once, could be a mistake, but constantly? Boy, did I ever misjudge Don."

"Did you hear Sheila say that she 'got even' with him?" Brian asked. "And then she added 'several times'. What do you think that meant?"

"I have no idea," Nedra said. "Do you have any thoughts?"

"I suspect that Sheila might have been getting a little on the side herself," he said.

Astonished, Nedra said, "No. Really?"

"It's a possibility. Unless she..." Brian didn't finish his sentence.

"What? Unless she what?"

He hesitated. "Nothing."

"Come on, you can tell your sister."

"I can't say. It's too farfetched," he said. "It's the lawyer in me looking for and finding the worst in every situation."

"You don't think she...no she wouldn't, would she?" Now it was Nedra's turn to let her sentence drop off.

Brian shrugged his shoulders. "You never know...a drop of something here, a drop of something there and voila, the cheating bastard's gone."

"You sure are cynical," she said. "Are you really talking about poison here?"

"I plead the Fifth."

Nedra shook her head. "All I can say is that I'm happy beyond measure that this mess is behind me and I can hand the duties of the trust fund over to you. As far as I'm concerned, I never want to hear about any of this again." Then she added softly, "The whole thing makes me sick."

Chapter 33
Lettie

It took a few hours, but Nedra eventually answered Lettie's text.

Sorry, I've been in Chicago with Brian most of the morning. Yeah, I can swing by when I get back in town. Give me about forty minutes.

Lettie responded.

Good. I'll be in the studio.

Time passed quickly as Lettie continued to work on her latest project. Before long Picasso heard something and sat at attention, alerting Lettie. She checked the time and assumed it must be Nedra. Opening the studio door, she welcomed her friend inside.

"What a day," Nedra said as she slid her coat from her arms. "I'm glad to be out of the city."

"What were you doing down there?" Lettie asked, and then said, "Want some tea?"

"I'd love some tea. Look what I happened to buy on the way home." Nedra spun a mid-sized brown box around so Lettie could see the unique Scone City logo.

"Scones!" Lettie said. "Tell me these are chocolate chip scones."

"Yes, ma'am. The best in the world."

Lounging in the studio's 'thoughtful place' with their feet on the battered coffee table, Nedra and Lettie purred over every bite of their scones.

"This is just what I needed," Nedra said.

"I'm sorry about what happened," Lettie told her. "I mean about being let go at work."

"I'll admit, it was a shocker. But once I got through the initial horror of being fired, I took stock of all I had going for myself and stepped away from the wallowing."

"You recover quickly, girl."

Nedra explained her day at the MQR interviewing the quilters and meeting Irma. "At ninety-eight years old she's fought her whole life simply to survive—to make life better for all of us women who came after her. Think about the changes she's seen and personally been through. She was two years old when women were finally allowed to vote. Her mother was a jailed suffragette!"

"No way," Lettie said.

"She inspired me so much, not only to get off my butt and stop feeling sorry for myself, but to rethink my book subject."

Lettie's raised eyebrows and tilt of her head signaled her friend to continue.

"I'm scrapping my original idea for now and thinking of a book that is a compilation of stories about quilts and quilters," Nedra said. "I'm talking about poignant stories with research and photos to back them up. I'd like to feature only quilters who have been passengers at the MQR."

Lettie couldn't imagine how Ned's book would be different from other books sharing stories about quilters. But Nedra hadn't finished clarifying her vision yet and her voice became more enthusiastic as she continued.

"Irma's mother taught her to sew and quilt, and then Irma passed on the passion to her daughters who also taught their daughters the power of needle and thread. Through all of their joy and sadness quilting prevailed much like it does for us today. It's part of who we are. Rich or poor…needle and thread binds us all together."

Nedra hesitated and Lettie sensed her friend was reluctant to say more, but after examining her manicure for a moment, she continued. "Have you ever thought that we are warriors, Lettie? Our strength comes from within—add the gift of creativity through quilting and we become self-assured and unstoppable. We are all warriors. We are quilting warriors."

"I like it," Lettie said, as she rubbed goosebumps that had risen on her arms.

"I don't have a word written yet," Nedra smiled, "but my book will be titled, *Quilting Warriors of the MQR.*"

"It sounds fabulous, Ned. If anyone can do it, I know you can."

Nedra appeared slightly embarrassed. "Thanks. I think I can, too." Slapping her hands on her knees, she said, "I've carried on long enough. What was it that you wanted to see me about?"

"I think it might have become a moot point," Lettie said.

"Why's that?"

"Let me start by showing you what I'm working on," Lettie said. "Follow me."

Intrigued with Lettie's ideas, Nedra eventually said, "I love the direction you're taking, but what does this have to do with me?"

"I was going to ask you if you'd like to collaborate with me. I thought you might want to write the patterns and the backstory for the pattern book." Lettie clearly saw surprise on Nedra's face. "I'm sorry, Ned. This idea came to me after I heard you were questioning yourself about writing a novel. I thought...well, never mind, it was silly of me."

Beaming, her friend said, "No, Lettie, this is perfect. Yes, I'd be honored to team up with you on this project. I'd love to work together."

"But what about the warrior book?" Lettie said.

"To start with," Nedra explained, "it will take quite a while for me to interview and research quilters for the book. But more importantly you could be my first warrior."

Lettie placed a hand on her chest. "Me?"

"Of course, it's a perfect fit. Your idea for this series of quilt patterns is such a unique approach and your artistic backstory is ideal," Nedra said. "I think we can give the quilter excellent and thoughtful patterns for your visions, as well as captivate them with your story." Nedra spread her hands wide. "Win. Win."

Lettie laughed. "I've always wanted to be a badass warrior."

Chapter 34
Nedra

Not five minutes from Lettie's house, Nedra's phone notified her through a chirping sound that she had received a text message. Thinking she had left something at Lettie's studio, Nedra pulled off the road and checked the message. It was a group message from Marge to all of the board members of the Mayflower Quilters Retreat:

>Emergency meeting of the board called by Brian tonight. 7 pm. I hope everyone can make it. It's about the eminent domain thingy.

"Brian called the meeting?" Nedra spoke out loud to herself. She'd spent all morning with her brother and he never said a word to her about a meeting at the MQR. She could hear his reason for not telling her...*Attorney-client privilege, my dear sister. You wouldn't want me blabbing your business to everyone, would you?*

No, she wouldn't. As a matter of fact Nedra had told her brother that morning that she was not sharing the Don, Sheila, Rita Kelsey fiasco with her friends. "Maybe someday," she told him, "but after keeping Don's secret for so long, I'm not ready to discuss the gory details with anyone."

Texting Marge back, she asked if dinner was included before the meeting. She was starved. Other than the scone she had eaten at Lettie's, nothing solid had passed her lips all day. The thought of a meal cooked by Chef Evelyn made her mouth water.

Marge's response was quick:

>Sure. Come on by.

After indicating a left turn, Nedra checked her mirror and entered back onto the road. The digital clock in the car told her she had enough time to make a quick stop at the

Quilter's Closet to see if any new fabric had arrived.

Brian was always prompt, and true to form he greeted the members of the Mayflower Quilters Retreat Board of Directors as they entered the conference room. Speculation ran high as the women theorized what the future held for their beloved retreat. With the exception of Nancy, who was still on her honeymoon for another three days, everyone had arrived on time—even Rosa.

Sunnie had situated her chair close to where her daughter sat. Nedra saw Mom reach over and hold Phree's hand under the table. Marge sat on the other side of Phree and she slipped her arm around her boss's back.

Warriors…all of us. Bolstering those who are down.

Brian stood. "Thank you all for coming on such short notice. Since this is an informal gathering, we'll dispense with the standard procedure for a board meeting. I'll get right to the purpose that we're here. As you have all assumed, this gathering has to do with the legal and final decision over the eminent domain notice that was sent out earlier." Brian looked down and took a deep breath.

Phree closed her eyes and bowed her head. Everyone in the room sat motionless, waiting to hear the verdict.

"The long and the short of is…" Brian hesitated and eventually lifted his eyes to look at Phree. A huge smile split his face. "It's over…we won!" He threw several papers in the air and as they drifted to the conference table the room erupted in laughter and relief.

Phree placed her head in her hands and shook with sobs as Sunnie bent over her daughter smoothing her hair while placing Mom kisses on Phree's head. Hugs, embraces, and tears were shared. Cellphones came out for photos and when Phree had finally recovered enough to raise her head off her arms, Nedra thought she'd never seen someone so happy be that red and puffy.

Walking toward her lawyer and friend, she met Brian halfway around the long table where they embraced. Phree disappeared in Brian's large frame. More photos were snapped and Nedra's chest swelled with pride for the brother she loved so much.

Pulling away from the hug, Phree said, "How did this happen? I thought once you received a notice it was a done deal."

The room turned quiet again as he explained. "It usually is printed in stone by the time the notices go out. But they made one crucial mistake."

"What was that?" Marge asked.

"It was that darn yaller line." Brian laughed. "Without that line on the map there would have been no proof of a second proposal and there wouldn't have been a thing that I could object to." Tracing his pointer finger through the air while tracing the imaginary line, he said, "It was easy to argue that the second proposal met all of the qualifications set forth to legalize the action of eminent domain, whereas the original proposal...the one which Phree received, was invalid by their own stated rules."

"I have no idea what you just said, Brian," Rosa called out, "but I'll take your word that it's good news."

"So we're good to go? We can carry on as usual? No land loss?" Phree asked.

"There is a little tip of your property on the southernmost edge that will be swept up for the bypass. But there should be no interference to the retreat, and yes, beyond that, it's completely over."

Several group photos were taken by Chef Evelyn to commemorate the MQR's freedom from an almost certain demise. Nedra couldn't count the times that evening when she heard congratulations, thank you, and I can't believe it. She thought of how surprised Nancy would be in three days when she arrived home from her honeymoon — there were many stories to tell but one secret to be kept.

Lettie approached her and they linked arms. Leaning against the wall they silently observed the festivities. Nodding toward the activity she asked, "What do you see over there, Nedra?"

After a short hesitation she said, "I see hope and pure happiness. I see my fierce women friends supporting each other. I see my brother and I'm so very proud of him."

They looked at each other, smiled, and Nedra added, "I see quilting warriors and nothing can stop them."

Peanut Butter Cookies with only Three Ingredients

18 cookies

Preheat oven to 350° Line a cookie sheet with parchment paper.

1 C. peanut butter

1 C. sugar

1 egg

Combine ingredients until smooth. Mix by hand or with an electric mixer.

You can simply drop dough by the spoonful onto prepared cookie sheet or form the dough into balls. In either case, place the dough about 2" apart. Use a fork to crosshatch the tops of the cookies or to flatten the balls.

Bake 6-8 minutes (but can take a smidge longer). DO NOT OVERBAKE!

Author's note:

Before baking, sprinkle a little sugar on top of the dropped spoonful or roll the dough balls in sugar.

You can use creamy or chunky peanut butter—your choice!

I've also seen people put a Hershey's Kiss on top before baking.

Karen is available for quilt guild talks, quilt shop talks, library talks, and book club discussions. She also offers a trunk show or bed-turning of her quilts. Contact her at **KarenDeWitt7@gmail.com** or by visiting her blog at **KarenDeWittAuthor.blogspot.com.**

Karen DeWitt is an avid quilter who holds an MFA in studio art. She is also a member of a Bunco Club that has been together for more than twenty years. Karen lives in the Chicago suburbs with her husband. They have one adult son.